OTHER TITLES BY ROY/ROY F. /RF SULLIVAN

Scattered Graves: The Civil War Campaigns of Cherokee Chief/ Confederate Brigadier General Stand Watie

The Civil War in Texas and the Southwest

The Texas Revolution: The Texas Navies

The Texas Revolution: Tejano Heroes

Escape from Phnom Penh: Americans in the Cambodian War

Reflections on Command: Kit Carson at the First Battle of Adobe Walls

Killing Fannin

Killing Davy Crockett

Murder at the Best Little Library in Texas

A Father Murphy Mystery: Murder at Mallow, Cork

A Jan Kokk Mystery: Gambol in Las Vegas

A Jan Kokk Mystery: Crises in Kerrville

A Jan Kokk Mystery: Who Killed Van Gogh?

A Jan Kokk Mystery: The Curacao Connection

A Jan Kokk Mystery: Murder Cruises the Antilles

KIA: Killed In the Alamo

Mayaguez and the Murder Ship

Titles are available online at sites such as Barnes & Noble Books,
Amazon Books,
Author House Books, et al.

THE RED BRA AND PANTIES MURDERS

AN ABBIE/BRUNO MYSTERY ROMANCE

ROY F. SULLIVAN

authorHOUSE®

AuthorHouse™
1663 Liberty Drive
Bloomington, IN 47403
www.authorhouse.com
Phone: 833-262-8899

Published by AuthorHouse 09/15/2021

ISBN: 978-1-6655-3754-4 (sc)
ISBN: 978-1-6655-3755-1 (e)

Print information available on the last page.

FOR NANCY: CRITIC, EDITOR, CO -CONSPIRATOR

PRINCIPAL CHARACTERS IN THE "RED BRA AND PANTIES MURDERS" IN ORDER OF APPEARANCE

Canyon Lake Police Chief Chester Rogers, Bruno's Viet Nam Buddy

Doctor Mills, Medical Examiner

Rose, Reporter for *The Canyon Lake Caller*

Abbie Brown, Designer/Decorator/Businesswoman, with designs on Bruno

Bruno Carter, Once her boyfriend, veteran, cowboy, now Brown's assistant

Lois Grimes, Abbie's chum and potential client at Canyon Lake

Hugh Grimes, Lois' missing husband, a sports car fanatic

Grace Woodley, Housekeeper and companion to Lois

Herb Glasser, President of the local retired officer chapter

Don Drake, Private investigator hired by Lois to find Hugh

Bernice Stone, the 'Lady in Red' found dead on a north beach

Alice- Sister of Grace, head of Lois' household

Eloise- Lois' sister, often substitutes for Grace at Lois' mansion

CONTENTS

ONE

CANYON LAKE

MONDAY A.M.

Chief of Police Chester Rogers grimaced as the Medical Examiner's van pulled beside his jeep in a swirl of hot dry Texas dust. It was a sultry day in the Texas Hill Country, no stranger to three digit afternoon temperatures.

Wordless, Rogers pointed to the yellow-taped patch of grass where the body of a young woman lay under the old olive drab army blanket usually carried in the Chief's jeep.

"A picnicking couple found her here about an hour ago," he pointed to the beach behind them. "What do you think, Doc?" He lifted the blanket from the body.

The body sprawled face-down, arms and legs spread, as if asleep in the sand.

“No signs of a struggle,” Doctor Mills observed. “Look at those bright red fingernails. I bet they’re recent painted.”

He made notations in his notebook. “Red hair, too. She liked really red. Unusual?”

“How old, do you think?” Rogers asked, looking over the ME’s shoulder.

Mills straightened up. “I’m guessing her age at between twenty five and thirty. No needle marks on arms. No ear lobe or tongue or nose holes for jewelry. That’s also unusual these days.”

The ME exposed labels on the bra and panties, her only clothing. “Whew, she sure dressed well. Both are marked with that expensive ‘Vicki’s Secret’ trade mark. Mail order only, I bet.”

The Chief looked up from his notebook. “You’re very well informed, Doc. Didn’t know you were expert in fancy lingerie, too. That may be very handy.”

Mills took a big bite from the tobacco plug extracted from his shirt pocket and chewed it a minute, studying the body of the young woman. He spat in the sand behind them.

“It’ll take me a while to give you a complete report, Chief. Rest assured I’m giving this young woman first priority. Luckily, there’s no one ahead of her.”

The doctor adjusted a straw hat to lessen the sunshine glare on his glasses.

He wiped the glasses with a tissue. "Got all the photos you need?" he asked the police photographer, who nodded.

"Can I take her now or do I have to wait?"

The Chief nodded. "All yours, Doc. Our photographer's made lots of shots. We initially turned her over so we could get a good photo of her face. I borrowed an artist from Missing Persons so we'll soon have a drawing of her face.

"Mum's the word, right, Doc. We haven't even started our investigation."

Rogers frowned at his admission. "Damn! Not even an ID as yet! Borrow, borrow, borrow. I even had to borrow an investigator from the county. Seems like we have nothing of our own in little old Canyon Lake. No money!"

Two overall-clad men emerged from the grey van, placed the body on a stretcher and lifted it through the rear double doors. Already in the passenger seat, Doctor Mills spat out the window, waved and saluted. "See 'ya, Chief."

Rogers opened the passenger door "I want that blanket back once you're through with it. Hopefully, there are clues on it. Don't forget now."

No sooner had the coroner's van departed, another vehicle, this one painted red, white and blue slid into the vacant place.

"Oh, Lord!" Rogers uttered as a female holding a microphone, scrambled out of the van, closely followed by a man shouldering a TV camera.

She grinned at the Chief's dour expression. "Look everybody! It's Roy Rogers!"

The more he detested the nickname, the more Rogers heard it, Rose, the reporter from the local newspaper, stuck the microphone in his face.

"What do we have here, Chief?" She nodded at the cameraman to go live. Then she noticed the body circled by the yellow flags at the beach.

"Murder, Chief? Drowning? Which is it? Who is it?"

He shook his head at the newswoman. "No comment at this time, Rose."

He retreated toward the body. "Stay out of the crime scene," he warned her.

"When's the press conference, Chief?" she yelled as he moved farther away. "This is a major news story! The public's got to know!"

Continuing to walk away, Rogers called back. "I'll announce one later."

Pausing beside a patrolwoman, he instructed her. "Keep everybody out of our crime scene."

"Yes, Chief."

Deputy Police Chief Tom Lorrance, standing in the hot sun, questioned the investigator borrowed from the county. "How's it going, Larry?"

Lorrance lifted a stained straw hat to wipe his forehead with a bandana. He nudged the investigator for a response.

Larry Francis looked up. "Been over the immediate beach area, but I want to do it again."

Rogers stepped over and asked the investigator.

"Already sent prints to the Texas Rangers, FBI, Missing Persons and Homeland Security," Francis recited proudly.

"Footprints"?

"No, sir. Any previous prints were obliterated by the high tide."

"Clothing? She had to be wearing something out here, more than bra and panties."

"Nothing found so far, Chief."

"What about personal effects, maybe a billfold? Needles, cigarette butts, trash of any kind?"

"Not a thing."

"Well, keep after it, Larry. There must be something here to give us a running start on this case."

Rogers turned to his deputy. "Tom, call the Highway Patrol operations desk and ask for a flyover looking for abandoned or suspicious vehicles--or anything unusual--within a couple of miles of here.

"How did the she get here?" The Chief smacked a hand against his pistol holster. "Somebody had to bring her to this lonely beach."

The Chief's phone sounded. "Yes?"

It was Betty from his office. "It's a madhouse back here, Chief. The Mayor wants a report right away. Are you returning soon?"

"Probably another hour until we've finished out here, Betty. Then I'm calling a get- together of everybody at the office to share what little information we have. Tell the Mayor we have no news for public announcement, nor even an identity! I'll call him as soon as I have something."

"Betty, can you work a couple hours overtime?"

"Sorry, Chief. I've got a sick baby at home."

"Okay. Then ask Constable Stevens to take over the phone duty. Sure hope your baby gets better. Looks like tomorrow may be another awful one, especially since we haven't identified our red-haired mystery lady with the red fingernails!

"Don't tell anyone, Betty, but her bra and panties were bright red, too. That's all she wore!"

TWO

KERRVILLE AND SAN ANTONIO

TUESDAY A.M.

The antique telephone in Bruno's aging farm house outside Kerrville, Texas, began clamoring for attention at six o'clock. He had been repairing fence with new cedar posts and barbed wire until dark the evening before.

"Howdy," he began, after clearing his throat. "If this is one of those robocalls about auto insurance, I'm hanging up!"

She giggled. "You just failed Course 101 in telephone courtesy, Bruno Carter. Bet you can't guess who this?"

He sat straight up in bed and swung out from under the sheets. "Say a few words," he cajoled.

"Dear Old Pampa High School," she began singing the lyrics of their old high school song.

He chuckled, turning on the table light with a free hand and whooping with delight.

"Abbie Brown! Is that still your name? I'd know that come-hither tone in your voice anywhere! Haven't heard it since you turned me down for that high school quarterback with the greasy hair. Hope you dumped him long ago, just like you did me."

"Would I be getting irritable you out of bed this early just to chat about high school? Yes, I'm still plain little Abbie, last-name Brown."

He grabbed levis from the floor and stood up. "As you damn well know, Abbie, I'd love to see you again! Remember I crowned you PHS Band Queen a hundred years ago?"

"Skip the high school stuff. I have a serious proposition, Bruno, and..."

He interrupted "Yes, yes, yes! Whatever you have in mind, I'm available!"

She laughed at his eagerness. "Get serious, Bruno. I'm making you a business, repeat, business proposition. Listen carefully. Ready?"

"Ready and willing," he boasted, "as long as it's legal and wholesome and involves you."

"Well, here it is, cowboy. I want to hire you for a few weeks, probably two, to drive us in my cranky old SUV to Canyon Lake. I know you are handy with a tractor so my SUV should be no problem for your Aggie skills. At the lake we have an appointment tomorrow to present my renovation and decoration proposal to a very rich lady, whom I've known since college. We were roommates there for four years.

"What's the catch, you're wondering? Knowing you are handy with cars and trucks, you ought to be able to fix the SUV if it breaks down, and get us there in time for my design presentation at 11:00 tomorrow morning. Besides, I think you'd be good company. We can play catch-up with each other after all these years. Sounds like fun, huh?

"Besides," she lowered her voice an octave, "we both need help now, at property and FIT time. I imagine you could use a little spare cash about now, right?

"I hear the beef market is down again. Your farm operation must be hurting, just like my design business.

"So I'm offering my former buddy--that's you--the chance to make some easy money. I can't tell you exactly how much you may earn since our client has yet to sign the contract we will propose tomorrow."

Abbie drew a breath. "Questions?"

Already, I was pulling on soiled sox and boots. I slowed. "You keep saying 'our' presentation. What do you expect from me?"

"Get to my studio at 245 San Pedro, San Antonio, as quick as you can. I mean PDQ! We'll have a sandwich or taco, drive my cranky old SUV to Canyon Lake, filled with all my charts, graphs and sample materials. Once there, we prepare to brief our client tomorrow morning at her fabulous residence on a big hill overlooking Canyon Lake.

"Are you with me, Bruno? Please say yes! I want to hear that door slam behind you. I guarantee you a profit, even if it has to come out of my pocket."

With that, I grabbed a toothbrush, fed the livestock and dog, called my marvelous, next door neighbor to please take over, grabbed Jeep keys and hobbled out the door.

Interstate 10 to San Antonio was not as crowded as usual and I made it to Abbie's business on San Pedro Street in record time. Record time, if you discount the heavy questions and doubts churning through my mind.

Was I doing this to accommodate an old friend whom I haven't seen lately? Or was I expecting to rekindle a serious relationship, interrupted by Viet Nam?

Every Christmas I received a card from Abbie Brown. Eight of them. I know since I keep them in an old El Producto cigar box in my desk drawer. Long ago I memorized her San Pedro address, checking each Christmas that neither her last name nor address had changed.

I pulled the jeep up into a broad, bricked driveway at 6565 San Pedro and whistled at its ranch-style grandeur. The two-story adobe and clay tile structure, surrounded by cactus, flowering plants and palms, looked business-like, yet elaborate. No way did it match my imagination of her place after all these years. Abbie had done well in her design business.

As I got out of the Jeep, she materialized outside a weathered yew doorway that looked like it had been taken from the Alamo. She was resplendent in grey business outfit and yellow silk blouse, topped by an auburn hair-do straight out of *Mademoiselle*.

I stopped to breathe deeply, feeling I'd forgotten to take my blood pressure pill that morning, which was true.

"Welcome, stranger," she grinned.

By then I stood at the door beside her. "Is it proper for the new hired hand to hug his new boss?"

I did so, before she could answer.

"Oh, Bruno! Am I glad to see you after all this time!"

I could see a great smile contesting with a flush line on her cheek.

"C'mon in, handsome soldier," she broke the trance. "Let's have a coffee or strong drink to settle us before ugly old business interferes."

I followed her through the massive door and whistled again. I don't subscribe to *House Beautiful* but I bet it didn't look as good as Abbe's office, work place, home, or whatever she calls it.

Inside, I grabbed an arm and turned her around. Wow! If I thought the work area area was stunning, it didn't compare with the Abbie I was holding just three inches away.

Her hair was tied in a sleek pony tail almost hiding a slender, tanned neck. Pearl earrings complemented the necklace and below, a delectable throat. Blue eyes and long black lashes challenged me for something beyond my clumsy embrace.

I sighed, trying to neutralize my feelings toward this new beautiful boss, who had just hired untalented me for some reason.

"Have a seat," she indicated a nearby couch while ringing a bell. A maid, smartly dressed in black skirt and white, starched apron, appeared.

"Two bourbons and water, Gwen, please. Remember now, Texas is currently in a drought."

Abbie opened a note pad and scooted away from me on the couch. Business had begun.

"You should begin by checking over our SUV outside, to be sure she'll make it to Canyon Lake. Why don't I buy a newer one, you wonder?

"The pandemic seriously dented my income and savings, as it probably did your farm operation.

"Right?"

I nodded while thanking Gwen for the tall brown-colored iced drink handed me.

"Never fear," I bragged. "That SUV will get us there even if I have to push her."

"My presentation is at eleven tomorrow morning," she reminded me crisply.

She glanced at her note pad. "Next item, sir. Please cram all my briefing materials and samples--and there's plenty of them in the hallway--into the SUV. Then we're ready to hit the road to our client's residence atop a beautiful, placid lake named Canyon."

She gauged my reaction. "Drink up, Bruno! We need to get cracking. See you outside."

I did a quick check of the SUV's oil, water, tires and gas. She looked old but serviceable, just like me. Canyon Lake was only an hour and half away, if all went well.

I jumped into the driver's seat as Abbie exited her office with a goodbye wave for Gwen. Reaching over her shoulder, I pulled her safety belt forward, over her shoulder and buckled it.

"Snug enough?" I asked.

"Fine, but too tight," she winced.

I loosened the belt, accidentally grazing her.

"In the future," she eyed me, "I think I'd better do the loosening and tightening. You bring back old memories and..." She stopped mid-sentence and changed the subject.

"How far are we from the lake?"

We were heading north out of San Antonio, on Highway 281. "We'll be there in less than an hour," I guesstimated. "How about filling me in on what you've been doing since old PHS?"

"You know most of it," she teased. "We were avid pen pals for the longest."

I turned to her "I'd rather hear your words. C'mon, tell me. Pick up with those years in that Austin school called T.U. which you attended."

She looked at me to see if I was kidding. Satisfied by my pleading look, she began.

"Lois, our future client at the lake, and I roomed together for four years. We were inseparables, both pledged to Alpha Zeta sorority. We helped each other with homework, studied together for exams, happily criticized each other's clothes and boyfriends.

"We truly were partners. After graduation we drifted apart, seeing each other occasionally in Austin where we both found jobs, me in design, Lois in real estate.

Eventually, she married a wealthy business man. You'll meet them both today at their fabulous hilltop house. 'House' isn't grand enough a description. It's a mansion!"

She nudged me "That enough?"

I wanted more of the personal variety. "Never engaged? Married?"

She pursed her lips. "Neither one. Here's were I'm supposed to say I was waiting for you, Bruno. It's been a long wait, hasn't it?"

I grimaced, turning off Highway 281 into a smaller paved road leading eastward to the lake.

She continued as I slowed down for a sharp turn. "My parents contacted the flu and passed several years ago, leaving me enough to start my own design business instead of working for someone else. I enjoy my work and somehow it's flourishing, despite the pandemic and economy.

"No engagement, no husband.

"That's it in a nutshell, Mr. Bruno, once of the faraway US Army. Now it's your turn. I want to hear you confess you've always been in love with me but Uncle Sam wouldn't let you go."

She pulled something out of a huge leather shoulder bag. “Hungry? Gwen made us sandwiches since our next real meal is a maybe.”

I was happy to accept a thick cheese and pickle sandwich instead of telling my ho-hum history. I noisily munched, too loudly to be heard.

Abbie had other ideas. “Go ahead, a bite here, a sentence there. Don’t hold anything back, including your romances with all those Red Cross girls, Army nurses and local knockouts.”

It was a weak alibi, but I tried. “There were so many, the telling would take several days, even weeks. Today, I want to entice, not scare you.”

She placed her hand on my shoulder. I liked it. “Nice,” I said.

“Begin Chapter One,” she instructed.

“Keep your hand there and I’ll outline the entire book.” I checked the rear view mirror for faster traffic.

“I went to College Station when you ran off to Austin. I was lucky to see you at those football games between our schools. Our college weekends were delightful but not nearly often enough for me.”

I stopped, realizing I was going too fast, both speaking and driving. Where was this heading?

“I confess,” brainlessly, I continued.

“You were constantly on my mind, making me study harder to keep up my grades. As the semesters passed, we saw each other less and less. I thought you were avoiding me.

"Somehow I finished the four years, got my diploma in one hand and an Army commission in the other.

"You were inaccessible during my training at Fort Benning. Then, suddenly I was on my way to Viet Nam. No time for letters, no contact other than an annual Christmas card.

"After discharge, I went home to the family farm. Both my parents passed, and I began upgrading my small beef herd. To support a larger one, I begin growing more hay, mostly hay-grazer, and feed. I was barely keeping wolves--in my case, coyotes--from the front door.

"This morning, you called me and I came running. Like always," I raised my hands in surrender.

She tightened her grip on my shoulder. "Let's work hard to convince Lois and Hugh Grimes to approve my design plans and sign our contract. We'll go from there. Okay?"

We entered the outskirts of the small town of Canyon Lake. "Know the way to that 'fabulous hilltop house' where we work?" I asked.

Abbie pointed to a big hill overlooking the town. "Right up there, partner. Right up there," she repeated.

THREE

CANYON LAKE

TUEDAY P.M.

Once in town, she pointed me to our destination on the hill. Although I previously programmed the Grimes' address in the GPS, I preferred her instructions. Her arm still encircled my shoulder and neck. Small successes at a time, I thought to myself.

Once on the hill leading to their residence at 101 Lake View Drive, I shifted to low gear, due to the increasing steepness of the hill.

The peak was higher than I imagined, seeing it from the town. It consisted of three distinct tracts. The first, where the transmission began stuttering, was named Hill Side Street. On it, a dozen or so two-bedroom houses were fronted by a combination of red brick and siding. Each sported a separate one car garage. All the roofs were of grey colored shingles. Lawns were small and several needed mowing.

Proudly, I thought of my own little farm house. It looked neater than these, at least to me.

The well-paved but steep road led to a second tier of houses. The street signs read Lake Overlook Drive. Here the houses were fewer, larger and farther apart. Brick construction still predominated but the colors were tan or beige unlike the uniform reds on Hill Side Street. Two-car garages were integral. Lawns were larger, and well kept, conforming to an association rulebook with fines and occasional inspections, I imagined.

Finally we were at the top of the hill. From Lake View Drive, we could see the entire eastern portion of the lake below us. The Grimes' mansion, as Abbie called it, was the largest and most imposing structure on the wide street. Neighboring houses looked smaller beside the opulence of the Grimes' place at 101. The garage looked big enough for three autos. A shiny new Lexus sedan was parked in the front driveway and I parked our veteran SUV beside it. The contrast between the two vehicles reminded me of our differences: Abbie, chic and appealing; me, rude and country.

Outside 101 Lake View Drive, jungle-like vegetation encircled the residence. You could imagine yourself in a tropical garden instead of the Texas Hill Country. The Grimes' gardener must have been from Hawaii since the verdant foliage surrounding the mansion spoke of Oahu rather than Comal County, Texas.

Abbie and I stood shoulder to shoulder, staring at the greenery as the massive front door which suddenly burst open. A nightgown-dressed female rushed out, her blue silk gown billowing behind as she grabbed Abbie with both hands.

"Thank God you're here!" She wept, almost wrestling my new employer to the pavement. I tried to separate the women, helping Abbie to her feet and fending off the other. I assumed she was Lois, our overwrought client.

Abbie tried to hold Lois closely while tearing off her own scarf with which to wipe Lois' tears. Abbie's questions were staccato. "What is it, dear? What's the matter? Are you ill?"

A white-apron clad woman, a companion or servant, came running out the front door to help Abbie hold the still-sobbing Lois upright. The trio, holding tightly to each other, embracing and weeping, reminded me of a tragic Greek drama.

Eventually, the one in the white apron gestured to the big house. "Let's get her inside." The three clumsily moved as one toward the big door which I opened widely.

"I'm Grace," the lady in the apron offered. "Let's get her inside on that big divan and I'll fetch her medicine. She's had quite a shock today."

Dumbfounded, Abbie and I sat on either side of Lois on a leather couch big enough for a basketball team. We stared at each other. Baffled, Abbie silently lifted her hands.

Lois was a short, well-built lady of 40 plus. Her hair contained so many reddish strands, it was difficult to name a predominate color. Her green eyes, common among the red-headed, passed over me without a bump. Something had shocked her, leaving her almost defenseless.

"What's wrong, Lois?" Abbie's question released a new dribble of tears from her old college roommate.

Grace was back with pills and water, kneeling before Lois, giving her the medicine, pill by pill. "I'll tell you," Grace said, between holding the glass for Lois to repeatedly sip.

"Mr. Grimes is missing! She doesn't know where he's gone and it's tearing her apart!"

"Missing?" I repeated dumbly. "Have the police been called? Does she need a doctor?"

A moment later, Lois wiped her mouth and seemed lucid, still clinging to Abbie with both arms, like a lost child.

"No doctor! No hospital!" She wailed, "I'm staying right here, in our home until Hugh walks through that door!

"I'll be alright," she gulped and stared at Abbie. "Only you must stay with me!"

Lois seemed aware of me for the first time. "Who's this?"

"That's Bruno, my good friend, dear. He's here to help with my presentation."

"Oh, yeah." Lois studied me. "Then he's okay." She raised her eyebrows at a new thought.

"You must stay, too, and help me find my husband! The police are doing nothing, not a damned thing to help!"

She immediately appealed to Abbie. "He will stay and find Hugh, won't he?"

Another thought caused her eyebrow to twitch. "My God!

"My husband may be lying in a ditch somewhere, unable to come home. He might be dying, or dead!" she screeched.

Eventually, Lois became quiet and fell asleep on the couch. Grace acted as our hostess, familiarizing us with the first floor, kitchen, pantry, and outside terrace. The place was immense. It could easily have held a small, rowdy political convention.

We ascended a wide staircase to the second floor. Grace pointed out an assortment of electronic security cameras, radios, telephones and televisions. "Mr. Grimes is very security-conscious, having lost a brother to intruders in his own home several years ago.

"Down this corridor," Grace gestured, "are your rooms. Ms. Brown, this is the room Mrs. Grimes selected for you because of the oleander tree you see outside that window. She recalls at school you were fascinated by a tree like this one, near your window.

"If this room isn't satisfactory, we'll easily find you another more to your liking. There are more than eight bedrooms like this in the residence."

Abbie looked at the room and rolled her eyes at me. "No comparison between this beautiful apartment and the tiny room Lois and I shared at college."

She tugged at my sleeve. "From blueprints, I had no idea how spacious these rooms were. This will do fine for me, Grace. Already, I feel like a visiting princess."

"Or queen," I interrupted. "Grace, I'm going to a local motel for the few weeks we'll be here."

"Oh, no, you don't, Mr. Carter! Mrs. Grimes was very specific. She wants you here so you and Ms. Brown's work will be uninterrupted. Your room is two doors down the corridor. Like Ms. Brown's, it has its own kitchenette, bath, study and outside balcony."

Abbie spoke for us both. "We're overwhelmed by the hospitality, Grace. We don't know how to thank you."

"You can thank Mrs. Grimes by helping her find that husband. She's frantic to find him!"

FOUR

CANYON LAKE

TUESDAY P.M.

On my way downtown to the police station, I stopped at a Texaco station to gas the thirsty old SUV. Business was slow since the station manager himself was out front and pumping gas.

"New in town?" His name tag read Ted.

"Fill her up?" Ted asked.

"Yes, to both, Ted. Thank you." I smiled, eager to gain information. "I bet you know most of the folks in town, right?"

"Pert near," Ted nodded.

"Bet you know Hugh Grimes," I challenged, fumbling in my new investigative role. Abbie, Lois and Grace had ordered me to town to ask questions about husband Hugh. My supervisors had increased from one to three in less than an hour in Canyon Lake.

Ted paused for a contemptuous spit. His knowledge of local people, even his own Texaco customers, had been challenged by an outsider.

"Sure, I know him. Rich man lives up the hill yonder," he pointed with a free hand. "Friend of yours, is he?"

"No, sir," I admitted. "A friend and I are visiting Mrs. Grimes. I bet you know her, too."

Ted shoved the gas hose back in the pump. "Yep, heard of her. Don't know her by sight. Don't think she gets out very much."

"Have you seen Mr. Grimes lately?"

"Matter of fact, I saw him twice the other night. He came by for some good old Texaco gasoline. Said he was lost and looking for Fifth Street. Later, I heard him shift gears in his sporty little red car and head out, fast, toward the lake. Does he owe you money?

Ted read the gas pump aloud. "Twenty-five seventy eight."

I handed him a credit card, following him into the station. "No, he doesn't owe me any money. Just hoping to find him, to chat about our service."

Ted handed me a receipt. "You were in the service? Which one?"

"Army. You?"

Ted leaned over the counter display of packaged candy, peanuts and gum. "I was in the Air Force. Korea, Pusan Air Base. Ever been there?"

"No, I never saw Korea, Ted. I was in Viet Nam and we didn't get out of country much.

"Thank you for your service, sir," I said. "If you see Mr. Grimes around, please ask him to call me at this number."

I gave him a card with my cell phone number.

Opening the door, I paused and turned around "Another question, Ted. Do you know the name of your local police chief?"

Ted frowned "Not in trouble already, are you?"

I chuckled. "No, I just got here! I'm not in trouble. I used to have a buddy named Rogers... Roy Rogers...although he hated that nickname. He claimed he was from somewhere here in the Hill Country. Claimed he wanted to become a policeman if he survived Viet Nam."

Ted studied me. "You're in luck then. He's our chief of police here. But I wouldn't call him 'Roy' Rogers. He don't like that name and he's big... mighty big."

"Which way is the police station?"

Ted pointed to a brown stone building two blocks away.

"Thanks, Ted," I climbed into the SUV. "Probably be seeing a lot of you while I'm here."

I waved out the open window and he waved back.

Black and whites occupied all the spaces in front of the weathered brown stone. A small yellowed sign over the front door announced this was the headquarters of the Canyon Lake Police Department. Instead of parking on a side street and jumping out, I took a few minutes, making notes on my conversation with Ted. Apparently, he knew most of the locals and didn't mind sharing his knowledge with a stranger.

Now I readied myself to question my old Viet Nam buddy, now Chief of Police Chester Rogers, about Lois' missing husband. This ought to be easy.

Rogers and I were Infantry lieutenant hooch-mates in Viet Nam. We shared a leaky squad tent containing two GI canvas cots, two also leaky air mattresses and, between the cots, a bottle of Early Times. That little tent was our bedroom, living room, snack bar and officer club. Our outdoor 'bath room' was a roll of toilet paper stuck on the handle of an entrenching tool, next to a distant and down-wind hole in the ground.

Basic, squalid? Sure, but an important reminder of where we hoped to return--upright if possible--after the war.

Would I recognize my old hooch-mate? Would we be strangers, staring at each other without remembering? At least I had a subject, the missing Hugh Grimes, with which to begin.

I walked into the police building and stepped up to the counter dividing inquirers from duty personnel. I had prepared a short question, in case Rogers didn't recognize me:

'Is Chief Rogers available? I need him to find a local missing man for me.'

That was my carefully prepared query, but I forgot it. My roiling memories of Chester, our exploits, screw-ups and responsibilities as rifle platoon leaders obliterated my prepared words.

I imagined I was standing outside our hooch and I had something to tell Chester, who was inside. I bellowed out in my fractured Vietnamese, 'TRUNG UY!' (Lieutenant!) to get his attention like I used to do.

An office door slammed opened. There stood my former brother lieutenant, now Chief of Police Chester Rogers.

He yelled. "Who said that?"

Staring at me in disbelief, Chester shook his head. "Is that really you, Bruno, you bastard? Is that really you, or am I dreaming? What the hell are you doing here?"

His tone softened as he beckoned me into his office. "It's okay, Doris. He's not dangerous. Coffee still hot? Two cups, please, for me and my old Army buddy!"

We stood inside his office, laughing like idiots happy to see one another, still alive on this side of the world. Hand shakes wouldn't do. We had to pound each other's backs, until we both were breathless.

Chester pushed me into a chair next to a big polished desk covered with paperwork and newspapers.

"What the hell are you doing here, Bruno? Never thought I'd see you again, after we landed back in the world at San Francisco."

I couldn't keep from grinning as we sat staring at each other. "You look great, buddy! Police Chief Rogers! Congratulations! Always knew you could do it."

We sat there for another minute, grinning at each other. Doris, his secretary, backed into the office holding a tray of coffee. I stood and took the big tray from her.

"Don't worry, Doris," Chester said. "This guy's harmless. We were in Viet Nam together a long time ago. Here we are, in good old Texas, U.S. of A. and still breathing!"

"Hi, Doris," I said. "I'm Bruno, the sane one. Thanks for the coffee."

She backed out the door as we sat sipping hot coffee. "Sure beats that instant coffee we used to make in the hooch," I began.

Chester's voice suddenly became sonorous, like he remembered he was the Police Chief. "Are you here after something, Bruno?" he questioned. "If so, you've come at a hell of a time."

He held up one of the newspapers on his desk. The headline, covering the entire top of the page in big red letters, screamed "WHO'S THE DEAD 'LADY IN RED?"

The second line of bold type beneath that read "HER IDENTITY BAFFLES POLICE WHO ASK FOR ASSISTANCE."

"See this?" Rogers slammed the newspaper on his desk. "Even the newspaper in San Marcos picked up this story. Austin, Dallas and Houston will be next!

"The mayor, the governor, the churches--everybody--want my head since we discovered her body late yesterday! I'm this close," he held up thumb and forefinger, "to being fired!"

Chester paused for a deep breath. "Now, what's your problem, old buddy, or is this just a social call?"

I swallowed and tried to smile, despite the red headlines. "Sorry, but I am here on a mission.

"Former hooch-mate," I began, "I'm in town with a lady friend, visiting Mrs. Lois Grimes, wife of local businessman, Hugh Grimes. We came here to present the Grimes a plan to renovate and redecorate that big house of theirs.

"Then Hugh, the husband, goes missing yesterday. The wife is frantic. She doesn't know where he is. Doesn't even know if he's dead or alive! Wants my lady friend and I to find and return her husband ASAP.

"The wife claims her telephone calls here have been unanswered. I fully understand your present dilemma with a fatality, no ID and the clamoring newspapers. Can your deputy--or anyone--fill me in on what you know or have done about Mrs. Grimes' missing husband?"

Chester sat behind his desk, his already red face deepening. "Think Viet Nam, Bruno! I'm being bombarded by 105 m.m. Howitzer rounds and you want me to come out of my bunker to investigate a hand grenade? I can't believe this!"

Quickly, I back-tracked. "Maybe I could just talk to your deputy or investigator about her missing husband? That will give me something to report to the wife, who is an old friend of the lady I accompanied here."

Chester moaned despite a grin, "Still chasing women, huh? Jeez, I hoped you had grown out of that stage by now.

"Tell you what I'll do for you, Bruno. I'll give you thirty minutes to talk and question my hard-working investigator about the husband. Remember the time you told the battalion commander I was at the aid station with hemorrhoids? Actually, I was playing poker with the captain and you took my duty. Remember?"

"So, thirty minutes with your investigator pays off that old debt to me?" I was incredulous.

"Roger that, Bruno." Rogers checked his wristwatch. "Your thirty minutes just started."

FIVE

CANYON LAKE

WEDNESDAY A.M.

It was early morning when I arrived back at 101 Lake View Drive. Everyone was in bed, except Abbie, who met me at the door.

Instead of 'I missed you. Come in for hugs and kisses,' her first words were "What did the police say about Hugh?"

I reviewed my notes taken at the station. 'Quote. Larry Francis, the Police Chief's investigator, is more concerned about a 'Lady in Red' newspaper headline than he is about our local businessman missing for less than 24 hours Unquote.'

I continued quoting the investigator from memory.

"He'll probably show up today after a few drinks at the corner tavern with old friends." Larry said. "Don't worry. May I call you Bruno?"

"Please do," I responded, anxious to gain an information-sharing police friend. "Have you tried to locate Mr. Grimes' sports car? Maybe he's in a ditch somewhere right now and needs assistance. What about area hospitals? Maybe he's in a coma somewhere."

"We put out a 'Be On Lookout' for him and his car, but no results so far," was the flat response. "Hospital searches have proved negative, too.

"As you can imagine, Bruno," he continued more animated, "a young female found dead at the lake is absorbing all our attention and resources. This unidentified 'Lady in Red,' as the papers call her, is dead, maybe even a homicide. Your Mr. Grimes is just another wayward husband, despite his wealth and social position. Maybe he went on a business trip out of town and his wife forgot. Or... he didn't tell her for some reason!" Larry raised his eyebrows suggestively, making clear his meaning.

Closing his notebook with a snap, Larry made a face. "The newspapers--even in Austin and Dallas--are hot on our butt. Dogging us, first to identify her, secondly, to determine what happened to her, the now famous, but unknown, 'Lady in Red."

I held up a hand to slow his dismissal. "His wife told me he was on his way to the bank Tuesday morning, when she last saw him. Larry," I smiled politely, "have you or anyone checked with the bank? Maybe a gas station attendant, bus station ticket taker…maybe a postman remembers seeing Grimes somewhere Monday?"

Larry examined his fingernails. "Help yourself, Mr. Bruno. Explore, inquire, even interview every one in town if you like. But if you find Grimes--or any trace of him-- notify me first. Not the damn newspaper! Understand? If you don't, the Chief will be all over you like an angry hornet! No kidding!

"He's already pissed that someone leaked to Rose, the local reporter, how the deceased was dressed when found at the lake. Now it's an oversized headline and lead story in newspapers everywhere!"

Abbie and I were having a quiet exchange in the Grimes' gigantic living room. An exhausted Lois was upstairs in bed, Abbie said.

I began my report. "In a nutshell, the police have done nothing about Hugh, except look for his sports car.

"It's going to be up to us to get out there and find where Hugh went yesterday morning when Lois last saw him. She thought," I emphasized, "he was going to the bank.

"So that's where we'll start."

Abbie nodded agreement.

"Any other ideas where we should go?" I asked.

"Well, Lois is active in the local flower and garden club, church guild and chamber of commerce," Abbie read from her notebook.

"I spent yesterday afternoon telephoning around those places for information and trying to console Lois. Neither attempt was successful. One lady at the local florist thought she had seen a little car like Hugh's at the gas station, but she wasn't sure when. I haven't checked the gas station as yet."

In a surprise mood, Abbie patted my unshaved cheek.

"Do that again," I pleaded. "You just motivated me to go to the bank and gas station. Want to come, Boss?"

"Sure. I'll just change shoes. Stop calling me 'Boss.' We're a team!"

I interpreted that as an invitation and kissed her cheek.

Wanting more, but I hesitated when I should have advanced.

"We need a statement from Lois authorizing us to examine their bank accounts. Think she's awake enough to write one for us, teammate?"

It worked, after I was chastised for kissing her cheek. We named the SUV 'Sally', boarded her, and left for the bank.

"Chief, we got a hit, although a little one!" Investigator Larry strutted into Chief Rogers' office. "Maybe this is small potatoes, but it's something!"

"Spit it out, Larry. What have you got?"

"Ticket seller at the bus station remembers a girl with red fingernails arriving on the Dallas bus late Monday night. She said the nails were very, very red as if she'd just painted them. The ticket seller was so interested in the damn fingernails, she couldn't otherwise describe the girl. Maybe that girl is our missing 'Lady in Red"?

"Did this girl have red hair?"

"Ticket seller didn't know. Girl was wearing a big scarf."

"A red scarf?"

"No, sir. Plain white. She did remember the new arrival asked where is Fifth Street and the ticket seller told her."

"What about a list of passengers arriving from Dallas?"

"They're looking, but can't find it. The bus station blames a new dispatcher."

"Keep digging, Larry, or you'll be digging both our career graves.

"Larry, did she remember where the girl went from there? Taxi? Someone pick her up? What?"

"Still checking, Chief. I'm on it."

"Okay. But Larry…"

"Chief?"

"Don't go blabbing this to Rose, that snoop reporter. Hear?"

The Hill Country State Bank, an aged red brick, one-story building, was directly across the street from the Church of Christ, as if each was protecting the other. Abbie and I walked in, after agreeing on our roles and approach.

"I'm Ms. Brown from San Antonio here to speak to the president." She sounded so professional, I wanted to hug her. Instead, I grinned at the president's winsome secretary.

"On personal matters," I chimed in, as the secretary nodded and buzzed her boss on the intercom.

Mr. Thornton, the bank president, hurriedly turned off the TV as we entered his office. He'd been watching 'The Price is Right."

"Yes, yes," he mumbled. "A personal matter is it? How may I help you, Ms. Brown and Mr…?" He looked at me. My levis and soiled snap button shirt made him leery.

"I'm Bruno Carter, Ms. Brown's assistant," I explained, still smiling.

Introductions out of the way, Thornton waved us to chairs in front of a battered mahogany desk.

Abbie extended Lois' handwritten letter. "We're close friends visiting Mrs. Grimes. Mr. Thornton, I'm sure you've heard that Mr. Grimes is missing since yesterday?"

"Ah, of course. Sorry to hear that. Is there any news about his whereabouts?"

Thornton held up a hand as he reread Lois' letter.

Once he finished, I answered. "No, sir. That's why Ms. Brown and I are here, to help locate him. Ms. Brown and Mrs. Grimes are close friends since college. So, Ms. Brown and I are here to assist her in any way we can."

"What may the Hill Country State Bank do for you?"

Abbie's turn. "Mrs. Grimes last saw her husband Tuesday morning. She told us he was on his way here to your bank. Was Mr. Grimes here at any time Tuesday? Did he transact any business here that day?"

I added. "Has there been any change in the Grimes' bank accounts since Tuesday?"

Thornton reached for the intercom. "Mr. Roberts, can you come to my office now? Please bring the accounts of Mr. and Mrs. Hugh Grimes. Thank you."

Thornton sat back, either committing us to memory or wondering who won the new sedan on "The Price is Right."

An older man limped through the door carrying two large ledgers. "Yes, Mr. Thornton?"

"This is Mr. Roberts, who is most familiar with the Grimes' checking and savings accounts. Ms. Brown and Mr. Carter here are seeking information about the Grimes' accounts. You may be frank in answering their questions."

He waved Lois' letter. "Unusual, I know but Mrs. Grimes instructs us to fully answer all their questions."

Abbie led off. "Mr. Roberts, did you see Mr. Grimes here in the bank yesterday?"

Roberts opened and studied one of the ledgers in his lap "Yes. Ms… Brown. Mr. Grimes came in early that morning and cashed a personal check for…" he turned a page, "ten thousand dollars."

"Was that an unusual amount?" I asked, wishing I were able to casually withdraw a like amount from my bank in Kerrville.

"No, sir. The Grimes enjoy hefty balances in both their accounts."

I asked "Which account was this check written on?"

"Their checking account."

Abbie made a note. “Has anything unusual happened in any of the Grimes’ accounts lately?”

“No, M’am. Their accounts are unusually stable.”

“Is there an insurance policy associated with their accounts?”

At a nod from Thornton, Roberts answered. “Yes, unless there has been a recent change. They hold quite large insurance policies, $500,000 on each of their lives.”

I nodded at Roberts. “Did Mr. Grimes appear agitated or act unusual when he was here Tuesday?”

Roberts pursed his lips. “He seemed particularly pleased. Even offered me a fine cigar.” He glanced at Thornton before adding, “I declined his offer, of course.”

Thornton smiled proudly. “Smoking is not conducive to the activities or atmosphere of a fine, people-caring bank such as ours.”

On our way out of Thornton’s office, I paused. “Has anyone asked if Mr. Grimes was here Monday? Perhaps the police?”

“No, there have been no inquiries other than yours.”

SIX

CANYON LAKE

WEDNESDAY

"Not much there, was there?" I asked Abbie. "But at least we know Hugh was here momentarily." she nodded agreement.

"Why did he want ten thousand from their account? What was the purpose?"

"Maybe a Caribbean cruise?" I joked. "A nice one, like the one we're going to..."

She punched me playfully on the chin. "Hold that thought, cowboy. We already have more cattle here than we can brand."

I tried to look solemn, instead of disappointed. "Maybe Lois has some idea why he withdrew that money Tuesday? Let's mosey over to the gas station," I copied her western accent.

"Why? Do we need gas?"

"No. Remember a lady at the florist thought she may have seen Hugh's sports car there? Maybe the 'Lady in Red' was at the gas station after she got off the Dallas bus?"

"Good memory, Bruno. Let's mount up and ride over there."

Doc Mills, the medical examiner, made a point of rapping loudly on the police chief's door before nine o'clock that morning.

"Come in," brayed Chief Rogers, drinking his second cup of Betty's coffee. "But only if it's good news!"

"A mixed message, Chief," Mills began waving a thin folder. "I worked until ten last night to get you this report on your 'Lady in Red."

"Not *my* 'Lady in Red!' But thanks for your usual quick and professional opinion. Was she…?"

"Drowned," Mills finished the sentence, wondering if he'd be offered a cup of coffee. "But, there's more." Mills paused, scratching thinning grey hair.

"Got a extra cup of coffee lying around here unused?"

"Betty!"

"Yes, Chief?"

"Got a cup of your famous coffee for the good doctor here?"

"Coming up!" She left the door open to return quickly with a steaming cup for Mills.

"Thanks, Betty," Doc winked at her as he took the hot cup.

After a trial sip, Mills opened the folder and sat down. "As I said, it's a mixed message, Chief. Death by drowning is my conclusion, with a small caveat."

Mills read from his report. "Her eyes were open and glaring, head leaning back, mouth open, no froth, indicating she'd not been in the water any length of time, red hair matted on forehead.

"Is that enough description for you? Irreversible cerebral anoxia..."

The chief interrupted. "What's that last thing mean?"

"Drowning."

"Then what's the caveat?"

"There is a slight contusion on one arm. She might have bumped it against something on the bus or anywhere. Not enough tissue damage to tell." He put his empty cup on the table.

Rogers nodded. "What about an autopsy? Will that reveal anything?"

"Autopsies are seldom performed in drowning cases, Chief. Doubtful it would give any insight about how the drowning occurred. Still, if you want one, I'll sure do it."

"I'd again like to look at those photos of the body and clothing that you have, Doc."

"Sure, but she was clothed only in bright red bra and panties."

"I know, I know, but laundry marks might be useful in determining her identity or home. We have nothing else to go on at the moment.

"If you don't mind, take your empty cup back to Betty."

Alone after the doctor left, Chief Rogers sat at his desk, rubbing his forehead. "What the hell do I do now?" he asked. "Go to the county sheriff, Highway Patrol and FBI for help? Was that poor girl's death an accident or was it homicide?"

Abbie and I wheeled into the Texaco gas station. Ted, the station manager, sat outside, watching the passing parade of pick-up trucks and occasional pedestrians. He grinned broadly as I waved at him and stopped the SUV beside a vacant pump.

"Good morning, Ted!" I got out and walked toward him. "Good to see you again. Remember me from yesterday?"

"Howdy, Mr…."

I finished his greeting. "Bruno. This is my boss, Ms. Brown," I gestured toward Abbie, who was checking her hair in the visor mirror. "You may recall Ms. Brown and I are here to assist Mrs. Grimes find her missing husband."

"Morning, Ms. Brown," Ted stood and lifted his straw hat. "Yep, the whole town's guessing about Mr. Grimes, why he's gone and where he went."

Her lipstick received the next mirror check. Abbie smiled at Ted and asked, "What do most people say about Mr. Grimes, Ted?"

"Nobody has a handle on that, M'am. Some folks say he maybe went to San Antonio, some say Dallas. I don't rightly know where. Haven't seen him and that little red car of his since I saw you last," Ted blinked at me.

"Fill her up?" he asked.

"Yes, please," I fished in my billfold for a credit card.. "Say, Ted, different subject?"

"Yeah?"

"Have you seen a young red-headed girl around here, or at the bus station, lately?"

"Can't help you, Mr. Bruno. Your SUV's sure thirsty." He read the pump amount.

"That'll be $10.45 for the gas.

"Wash your window? Maybe cold sodas for you and Ms. Brown?"

"Thanks, but we just had coffee."

"Am I remembering right?" Ted asked. "Weren't you in the Army?"

"Guilty as charged, Ted."

"Well, are you a member of that retired officer group like we have around here?

"Yes, also guilty," I quipped.

Ted pulled a wrinkled paper sack of chewing tobacco out of a hip pocket. "So was your Mr. Grimes. Once he was the president of their local chapter, or whatever you call it."

"Interesting. Thanks, Ted. Guess Grimes has lots of friends in that same chapter. Do you know any of their names? I'd like to talk to one or two of them."

Ted spat on the pavement. "Try Herb Glasser. He's in the phone book. That guy loves to relive his service days."

"Thanks again, Ted. I'll give him a call."

Abbie closed her notebook as we drove away. "Who were you talking about?"

"A member of the local retired officers' association. Write down Herb Glasser in your notebook, please, in case I forget."

"Sorry, chum," she patted my shoulder in a now familiar gesture. "We've discovered very little new today."

"At least we have the name of another contact. We'll ask him about Hugh."

Abbie wrote the name in her notebook. "Where now, knight in shining armor?"

I squeezed her hand. "I see a garage down the street. What say we ask there? I bet they are well acquainted with Hugh's little red sports car. Red seems to be his favorite color, doesn't it?"

"Red, red!" Abbie murmured. "All I hear is red, as in code red. What's that mean, anyway?"

"I think it means a fire, or maybe the red color of fire, like our 'Lady in Red' at the beach."

I didn't know if she accepted my definition or the suggestion that we go to the next-door garage. I took a chance and stopped the SUV beside an open garage bay.

The big yellow and green sign outside read, 'The Ray Noble Garage. If We Can't Fix It, Better Buy a Horse."

A Mazda Miata was being serviced by a young, broad-shouldered mechanic wearing overalls.

"Can I help you?" He eyed 'Sally,' our aging SUV doubtfully.

"Please," I peered into the Miata's open hood. "Any idea how fast this baby will go, all-out?"

"No, sir," he replied. "I don't drive them, I just fix them."

"I bet you work on a lot of sports cars around town."

He wiped his hands on a piece of waste. "Not only those in Canyon Lake, but all over the Hill Country.

"I'm Bobby Noble. My dad, Ray, owns this garage. As our sign says," he pointed, proudly, "if we can't fix it, you're better off with a good horse."

We shook hands. "Glad to know you, Bobby. I'm Bruno from Kerrville. Ever worked on a little red sports car here? I don't remember the make but I hear it's in town a lot."

"Sure 'nuff! I know that car. It's a flashy red Spyder owned by Mr. Grimes. I've tuned it for him lots of times. He fixes it, brings it in and I re-fix it."

"Seen it recently? I've been trying to contact him for several days."

Bobby scratched his hair, "Isn't he the guy who is missing? Everyone's talking about him."

"Yes, sir. That's him. Remember when you last saw him or his red car?"

"Been weeks since he's been here for anything. Funny, the police were here, asking the same question yesterday. Maybe they can tell you about him."

After thanking Bobby, I crawled into the SUV beside Abbie. We frowned at one another.

"No luck here, either, Boss. Let me buy you lunch at that barbeque place we passed on the way here."

I'd noticed a 'Bill's Barbeque' café on the way to town.

"Don't tell Lois," Abbie fake-whispered, "but I could sure use a cold beer with that barbeque about now."

"She's not a teetotaler, is she?

"No, but apparently, Lois loves her homemade margaritas!"

We chose a well-worn picnic table, sat side-by-side on its bench and admired the old soft drink, beer signs and out-of-state license plates festooning the walls.

She reminisced, "Reminds you of old Pampa, doesn't it?"

"I remember that Coney Island cafe on Cuyler Street best." I pulled paper napkins from the container on our table. "Hot dogs, chili all over it, topped with plenty of diced onions. Great eating!"

She nudged my hip. "We are not making much progress in locating the missing Mr. Grimes, are we?"

I agreed. "Does Lois talk about her husband much?

"Hardly ever," Abbie replied soberly. "Maybe Hugh doesn't want to be found. Did you consider that?"

I pointed at the menu chalked on the wall. "Or maybe, he's no longer with us?"

She studied the menu. "How about today's blue plate special? Ribs and potato salad?"

I licked parched lips. "You just sold me, Boss, if we throw in a cold beer or two."

Abbie mused about our lack of success. "Why don't we get some posters printed with Hugh's picture? Pass them around town?""

A pretty high school-aged waitress took our order and turned to go.

Abbie held up both hands. "Wait," she said, fumbling in her bag.

She held up a photo of Hugh recovered from the bag. "Know this guy?"

The waitress leaned forward to study it. "No, M'am. Never saw him in here."

"Or anywhere in town?" I added.

"No, sir. Never seen him anywhere."

I patted Abbie's ring-less third finger, left hand. "Nice try. Don't give up."

She answered immediately. "Never!" she cried. "We've got to help poor Lois!"

"What about those new interior design plans we were going to present poor Lois?"

Picking up a barbequed rib, she smacked her lips. "Later, handsome soldier! First things first!"

We stopped by a print and stationery office store and had two hundred posters printed with Hugh's photo. Our poster read;

HELP US FIND MISSING BUSINESSMAN
HUGH GRIMES, AGE 55,
OF CANYON LAKE.
$500 REWARD OFFERED FOR ACCURATE
INFO LEADING TO FINDING GRIMES

Abbie nodded at our wording. “Whose phone number shall we list?”

“How about my cell phone, Boss?”

She grabbed my shirt, pulling me over to her. “Okay about the phone, but no more of that ‘Boss’ stuff, remember?”

After beer and barbeque, we purchased a big stapler and spend the rest of the afternoon putting posters on every telephone pole, fence, bus stop and in the windows of every willing downtown business we could find in two hours.

“There’s a place we haven’t tried,” I winked at her.

“That bar,” I pointed. “We’ll give them a poster and our thirsts until six o’clock. Okay with that, former Boss?”

“Agree!” Abbie gloated, almost--but not quite--biting my ear.

SEVEN

CANYON LAKE

WEDNESDAY P.M.

That evening I helped Grace prepare fish tacos on the outside grill while Lois and Abbie relaxed on an oversized sofa in the living room.

"Tell me about him," Lois nodded at Grace and Bruno, both laughing and brandishing tongs at each other like fencers.

Abbie pursed her lips. "What would you like to know? As you can see, Bruno's a good ole country boy in need of a haircut and new levis."

"I mean his background. I know why he's here, helping you. Have you known him long?"

"Since the sixth grade at Sam Houston Elementary. You could say we've been friends a long time, huh?"

Lois lit a cigarette, still staring at Bruno. "What about now?"

"He has a small farm and runs stock near Kerrville. He returned there after Vietnam. I think he's cute, reliable, quiet, a bit of a loner with probably a smallish bank account and…"

"Stop, silly!" Lois held up a heavily-diamonded hand. "I mean, is he married?"

Abbie turned to again study Bruno standing behind the grill. "I'm trying to imagine Bruno being married."

That thought has occurred to her often of late, she admitted only to herself.

She answered, "We're just friends. We were 'steadies' way back in high school for the longest."

Puzzled by Lois' sudden interest, Abbie turned to her. "Don't tell me you're interested. You're not even a widow, unless there's terrible news you're keeping from me. Is there?"

Lois clapped her hands and chuckled. "That question proves how silly you are! Goodness, my only news comes from you and Bruno. As you've told me time and again, nobody knows where he is or has seen him since Tuesday. The police seem to care less and less about my missing husband. I think they've forgotten all about Hugh.

"I'm desperate for news, Abbie! At night my choices are to scream or drink more bourbon. This evening I hoped we could talk about something new. Sorry I asked about your boyfriend."

"He's not my boyfriend."

"Okay, okay! Speaking of something new, have you seen this latest catalogue of spicy lingerie?

"This'll take your mind off humdrum. It came in the mail several weeks ago and I haven't been able to put it down or throw it away. It's full of terribly tempting stuff!"

Lois opened the catalogue to a page of models posturing in skimpy underwear. "Just look!"

Abbie nodded, took the catalogue, absently placing it on the coffee table to examine later, if Lois mentioned it again.

She changed the subject. "Dear, have you personally spoken to the police chief lately about Hugh? Bruno and I have questioned several people who know Hugh. No one admits to seeing him since Tuesday, except the Texaco man.

"I just thought it might be useful for you to call the chief and again strongly express your…chagrin with the progress of his investigation."

Lois lit a cigarette and watched the smoke ascend to the twinkling crystal chandeliers above her. "I'll try the chief again, dear, but I'm thinking more and more about taking positive action myself."

Lois stubbed out the cigarette and turned to Abbie. “You live in San Antonio, dear. I bet you know a lot of professional people there, like yourself.”

Wondering if Lois was about to ask for a medical referral, Abbie nodded. “Sure, after almost fifteen years there I know lots of medical professionals. Need some helping sleeping soundly after Tuesday? Maybe you need a sleep specialist or even a psychologist?”

Lois lit another cigarette with shaky hands. “No, dear. An honest investigator…or a good detective is what I need.”

EIGHT

CANYON LAKE

THURSDAY

It was only seven-thirty in the morning, but Chief Rogers hadn't had his second cup of coffee yet.

"Where's that coffee, Betty?" he yelled, wiping his mouth with the back of a hand..

"Coming, Chief," she cried. "I had to run to the store. We ran out of coffee since you were here all night draining our last pot."

"Okay, okay, but hustle, please. While you're at it, call my ex-buddy, Bruno Carter."

"I don't have his number, Chief."

Rogers fished in a desk drawer for the card given him Tuesday.

"Yah, yah. I got the number here. I'll call him myself."

After several rings, I picked up and answered. “Carter here.”

People had been responding to us since six o’clock after we stapled up the posters with Hugh’s photo. Everyone claimed the $5,000 reward offered on the poster. No one knew Grimes by sight. None could positively say that the person they saw downtown Tuesday was Grimes. Still, my phone rang every few minutes.

“Smart-ass Carter here,” Rogers mimicked my crisp greeting

Rogers’ ire was up. “Listen up, you loose cannon! You should have checked with me before tacking those posters with Grimes’ photo all over town! This is not a game, former buddy!

“This is a murder investigation. I am the chief of police and I am in charge!”

I inhaled loudly. “Former buddy, am I? I’ve gathered more information about Hugh in thirty minutes than your investigator has all week! I even intend to share the reliable stuff with him!

“What about you?” I vented. “Have you received any leads from those artist pictures of the dead girl? If so, you sure as hell didn’t share them with us!”

Rogers’ angry retort caused Betty to close his door.

“If you do another dumb ass stunt like this, I’m arresting you for evidence tampering.” Rogers threatened. "Also, I'll put your sorry ass in jail! Got it?"

The chief slammed his phone down so hard, the windows rattled.

One question all callers asked me was "How do I know you won't use my information and then forget my reward?"

My answer: "If the information you give me turns out to be useless or inaccurate, you get no reward."

Abbie busily made notes from calls when I nodded at her. After several hours of bogus claims, her notes only covered a half page.

My phone rang again. "Carter here."

"Is this where I call to claim the $5,000 reward?"

"It is," I answered, "if your information leads to the whereabouts of Mr. Grimes.

What have you to report about Grimes' location?"

"I saw a man who looked like that photo on the poster."

"Do you know Grimes?"

"Well, no."

"What makes you think it was Grimes?" I shook my head at Abbie, ready to take notes. At my motion, she relaxed.

The caller answered "'Cause it looked like the man on your poster."

"Sir," I had said it so often it seemed automatic, "if you cannot positively identify the person as Mr. Grimes, your information is useless. Where and when did you see this person?"

"It was Saturday night at the pool hall. When do I get the reward?"

"Sir, you don't get the reward unless your information helps me find Mr. Grimes. Your info doesn't meet the criteria, so you don't get the reward. Thank you for calling."

"So it goes," Abbie poured them both fresh coffees. "Chief Rogers seems pretty upset with us, didn't he?"

"Yep, with me in particular. Too bad, since we once were great friends."

"If we had some good trading information, what would you want from him in exchange?

I squeezed Abbie's hand, surprised she didn't withdraw it. "What's our bargaining chip, lovable Boss?"

"The identity of the 'Lady in Red' and don't call me Boss!"

NINE

SAN ANTONIO

THURSDAY P.M.

"Telephone for you," Grace handed the phone to Lois sitting beside the pool. "A Mr. Drake?"

Lois nodded, taking off her sunglasses. "Lois Grimes, Mr. Drake. Thank you for returning my call so promptly. If you're a true San Antonioan, calling Canyon Lake is akin to telephoning the moon."

Drake chuckled politely He had just read an impressive personal file on her borrowed from a Department of Public Safety friend. It included an estimate of the Grimes' estate, a whopping seventeen million dollars.

"Not at all, Mrs. Grimes. I often visit the Hill Country. Your lack of traffic plus natural beauty beat Old San Antonio every time. After a visit there, I must force myself to return to work here."

Drake took a breath. The polite chatter over, now comes business, he thought.

"How may I help you, Mrs. Grimes?"

"Friends in the DPS highly praise you as a discreet, competent detective, Mr. Drake. I would like to discuss your possible help in a private matter. I'd rather not discuss the problem over the phone."

Drake reacted quickly, thinking hoorah! A wealthy client with a personal problem! "Perhaps we could meet at your convenience, Mrs. Grimes, and discuss your situation. Are you available…say, tomorrow afternoon or evening?"

"That would be lovely," Lois purred, "if not terribly inconvenient for you."

Drake checked the note he'd prepared before this call. "I have your address as 101 Lake View Drive in Canyon Lake. Would three in the afternoon be convenient?"

"That's terrific, Mr. Drake. You're very accommodating! How refreshing! Yes, to both the address and time. I look forward to seeing you."

Her last phrase was delivered in a business-like, yet intimate, tone making Drake even more pleased.

TEN

CANYON LAKE

FRIDAY

Abbie and I had an early breakfast with Lois by the pool. "You're up early, dear," Abbie put down the morning newspaper to greet her friend.

"Well, I have a visitor coming this afternoon who requires some serious preparation."

I selected a chocolate covered doughnut and asked, "About Hugh? Perhaps," I looked at Lois, then Abbie. "We should delay our trip to San Antonio today if this visitor has news."

"No, no," Lois motioned for Grace to pour more coffee. "Please don't change your plans, you two. I don't expect any news. This is just a little business inquiry."

In the SUV on our way to San Antonio, Abbie patted my cheek. "Who do you suppose she's seeing? A mysterious visitor… male I bet, since it's about business. Lois was once more open, at least to me."

I nuzzled her hand. "I hope he's the bearer of good news about Hugh's disappearance. Our questioning of the folks around here has been zero productive."

Abbie moved the hand to my shoulder. "Agreed, but we need to get back home to check my business and your farm. We've been away from our real dollar and cents worlds for several days."

I turned to study her. "Are we still going to brief your design proposal once Hugh is found?"

"Sure. That's our secondary mission here. Helping Lois find Hugh is still our primary. Reminds me, you never answered my question about how we might profit from Chief Rogers if we identify the 'Lady in Red' for him?"

I took a chance and patted her free hand. "Do you really think we can ID her?"

"I confess I haven't told you about an idea I'm anxious to try. What quid pro quo do we ask from your buddy, ole 'Roy' Rogers?

"By the way, did you give him that nickname?"

"Everyone in Viet Nam had a nickname, dear. Some were nice, like 'Roy Rogers,' others not so nice."

"What was yours?"

"Bruno, the bitcher, was the nicest."

She smiled. "Some night with drinks and a cozy fire, I want to hear the entirety of that confession."

Her playful tone changed. "You still owe me an answer, remember?"

"Sorry I didn't get back to you sooner but the answer's been a burr under my saddle blanket."

She punched my shoulder. "Am I just another burr, cowboy?"

I quickly checked traffic, slowed and managed to kiss her cheek.

"Well…I'd like to get our hands on any classified records the DOJ, missing persons or FBI has on Hugh. There must be something there we're missing. He seems too nice, almost angelic.

"So that type of records--the seamy stuff if it's there--is what I want from Chief Rogers. His murder investigation is as dead in the water as our famed 'Lady in Red,' still without an ID."

Abbie inched closer to me on the SUV's big front seat "Then after we finish our chores at my business and your farm, we'll confront your old buddy."

"We make a good team," I agreed and speeded up.

In Canyon Lake that afternoon, Don Drake, dressed in a conservative grey suit and blue tie, arrived at 101 Lake View and parked his Mercedes beside the Grimes' big Lexus.

Knowing the visitor's appointment time, Grace opened the door as he drove up. "Welcome, Mr. Drake. Mrs. Grimes awaits you in the dining room. Follow me, please."

Drake glanced around the big house approvingly. The report on the Grimes' finances must have been accurate, he grinned.

Lois sat at a large dining table, complete with notebook, pen and a silver coffee service.

"You're exactly on time, Mr. Drake. I admire that," she extended a hand.

He bowed slightly, accepting her hand. "Thank you for your welcome as well as those very explicit directions on how to get here."

"Thank Grace, my exceptional companion, for the directions. Shall we have coffee, Mr. Drake or would you prefer a drink?"

"Coffee, please, and call me Don."

At this, Grace poured two cups, smiled and departed, closing the door behind her.

Once Grace was out of the room, Lois studied her visitor carefully, noting his impressive professional and personal, appearance. Satisfied, she carefully began a summary she prepared and rehearsed last night.

She eyed Drake. “Private and confidential?”

“Private and confidential,” he assured her.

She drew a breath. “My husband Hugh, as you may have heard elsewhere, has been missing since Tuesday morning. I fear for his safety. He’s never done anything like this before. He is physically and mentally sound, his local physician says. He seldom drinks and never excessively. He drives a little sports car… yes, carelessly at times. The car is missing, just like Hugh.

“Law enforcement hereabouts consists of a small police department in town. The police chief, named Rogers, is the typical small town cop. He’s been absolutely no assistance in locating Hugh for me.

“I’m told that Rogers is over his head in another case of a young female found drowned in our local lake. The female has yet to be identified, another example of Chief Roger’s incompetence.

“I urgently need you to find my husband, Mr. Drake. This isn’t like him. I’ll pay whatever fees you charge for the search plus a hefty bonus for bringing Hugh home.

"Neither the local police nor my two San Antonio friends here to help me have succeeded. Were I you, I'd start with the State Police, FBI. Homeland Security and missing persons. Skip the locals.

"Admittedly, Don," she stopped to wipe tears with a handkerchief, "that's not much to go on. Will you find my husband, please?

"I must tell you that I have two friends living with me at the moment who are also trying to find Hugh for me. My old college roommate, Abbie Brown, and her assistant, Bruno Carter, have been trying to trace him for several days. They might be able to give you some ideas."

Drake wrote their names in his notebook. "I think I saw them leave as I was arriving at your front door. They were driving an SUV?"

Nodding, Lois took a deep breath from her unnerving recital. At this point her tears became a torrent. Lois lowered her head to the edge of the table and sobbed.

Drake rose to seek help from Grace in the kitchen. "Mrs. Grimes is not well and is weeping while telling me a problem. Can you please help her?'

Her face tense, Grace demanded, "What did you do to her?"

"Nothing," Drake insisted. "She told me about her husband and began crying. Is she on some kind of medication?"

"No. I think she just needs rest. I'd better take her upstairs to her room."

Grace eyed the well-dressed Drake. "Is your business with her over? It must have frightened her."

"Well, I think our initial discussion is through. Should I stay to make sure she's alright? Maybe she needs a doctor?"

"She'll be fine by morning, Mr. Drake. Thank you for your concern. Have you a message I can give her in the morning?"

"Yes, Grace." Drake gave her his business card. "Please tell her I'm working her case first thing tomorrow. In fact," he looked at his watch.

"I'm returning to San Antonio to start it now. I'll call her tomorrow with an update, hoping she's better."

"Good night, Mr. Drake. She…we…desperately need your help!"

ELEVEN

SAN ANTONIO

SATURDAY A.M

"What's that you're reading so carefully?" I asked, peering from a soft lounge chair in Abbie's expensively decorated office in San Antonio. Returning from shopping for new clothes for me, followed by a Mexican dinner with double margaritas, we felt well-fed and relaxed in familiar surroundings.

"Oh, it's a new lingerie catalog, one I borrowed from Lois yesterday.

"See?" She held up the color cover, dominated by models in scanty costumes.

"Lois orders her expensive lingerie from it. It's the same brand the drowned girl wore."

"Triple X!" I exclaimed. "Save that catalogue! Now I know what you are getting for Christmas.

Am I going to enjoy watching you unwrap multiple gifts from that catalogue, and model each item! Up close!" I added with a glint in my eye.

Giggling, she collapsed beside me on the lounge "Stop that! This is how I hope to identify our mysterious 'Lady in Red.' I think her underwear all came from this pricey catalogue, just like Lois' lingerie. I'll call the order desk with item numbers, colors and sizes.

"Maybe, just maybe," she thumped my chest for emphasis, "they can tell us who ordered them, plus that customer's address!

"Voila! We have the dead girl's identity to hand your fumbling police chief on a silver platter. In return, he gives you access to all those classified files you think will help us find Hugh Grimes."

I held up a cautionary hand. "How can you identify the item, color and size of the girl's clothing? You haven't even seen them."

"Keep up with me, cowboy," she chucked my chin. "I borrowed the drowned girl's red bra and panties from Doctor Mills, our friendly Medical Examiner!

"Now" she whooped, raising her hands like a winner, "hand me that phone."

The Drake Security Agency on Crockett Street, San Antonio, was open very early that morning.

Don Drake had called his deputy, Clive, at his home the night before to outline the information he needed by morning.

"Sorry to disturb you at such a late hour, Clive, but we need to get cracking by morning on a new--and I intend--highly profitable new case."

"No problem, Chief. This gives me a chance to turn off the terrible TV news. Who's our new client?"

"Mrs. Lois Grimes of Canyon Lake. I just visited at her home yesterday, which is a palace, more than a home, I might add. We need to pull out all stops in gathering information on her husband, one Hugh Grimes, successful businessman of Canyon Lake. He's been missing since Tuesday.

"Local cops are attempting to find him without success, probably pursuing the high road with state police, FBI, and the like.

"Somehow his name rings a bell. We'll explore the low road. I want you to ask your shifty South San Antonio sources for any info they can gather on Mr. Grimes' darker side. Taverns, bars, dance halls, wherever ladies congregate to meet out-of-town clients looking for a good time in our fair city. Grimes may be a convention attendee and you know about them. Parties in hotel rooms, escort services, expensive bars and restaurants, are the favorites of those guys. They're like tigers released from their cages to forage for food…or companionship." Drake winked.

"Am I being obtuse?"

"Clear as always, Chief. We'll get right on it and have a file we can start on by morning."

"One other thing, Clive. Two friends of our client have been trying to find her husband for the last few days. They drive an old battered SUV, Texas plates, and live with our esteemed client, so that's where the SUV is parked.

"Might be useful to know where these two amateurs go, probably muddying the waters for us. Put a bug under that SUV's fender so we can track them wherever they go. Those two amateurs won't outfox us!"

"Consider it done, Mr. Drake. Nobody's getting the big payoff but us!"

"Thanks, Clive. My best to your wife! She may not be seeing much of you these next few days if we're successful."

"Good night, Mr. Drake."

TWELVE

CANYON LAKE

SATURDAY A.M.

Abbie and I competed by singing snatches from our old high school song all the way to Canyon Lake.

"Let me call you sweetheart, I'm in love with you,
"Let me call you sweetheart, I will be true blue,
"Keep your colors flying as we stand by you,
"Dear Old Pampa High School,
we will see you through."

"You cheated!" Abbie objected. "You made up some of those words. I remember them all very clearly, like it was yesterday when you crowned me 'Queen of the PHS Band."

"I remember it well, too," I retorted, "because at the very moment I crowned you band queen, you were thinking about that greasy-haired football quarterback. I didn't stand a chance, did I?"

She playfully bit my ear. "What do you think now, cowboy?"

"I think you are one mighty fine investigator, able to identify that drowned girl at the lake. Nobody else was able to do that."

"I meant, what did you think in high school? You gave up too easily, Shorty."

"Why do you call me that?"

She rolled down her window for breeze. "If you don't stand tall, you won't get those classified materials we need. Number One, find Hugh. Number Two, get my design presentation back on center stage.

"That police chief, although you think him a chum, has you completely buffaloed. If you're not careful, you'll give him the name of the 'Lady in Red,'--that I discovered by persistent initiative--and you'll get none of the classified info we need in return."

I parked the SUV beside Chief Rogers' car, turned off the engine and stared at Abbie. She wore a frilly blue frock that clung to her slender figure, leaving nothing to my over-active imagination.

I gulped before being able to speak. "I'm about to make you eat your words, Boss. We'll see who's the taller, him or yours truly, in just a few minutes."

Inside police headquarters, I strode up to the counter. "Here to see the Chief!" I announced to the officer standing behind it.

"Abbie and Bruno," I answered the man's questioning look.

"Confidential police business," Abbie added sternly.

Her look got us through the chief's door in record time.

Rogers angrily looked up from reading the morning paper and drinking a cup of coffee. He yelled, "Who let these strays in here?"

"That did not sound like a 'Serve and Protect' greeting to me. Did it to you?" I nudged Abbie.

"Sit and have a coffee, you two, would be a much nicer welcome." Abbie chided as she got comfortable, seated in front of the chief's desk.

"This better be good," the Chief warned, buzzing Betty on the intercom. "Two coffees, please."

I stood in front of Chester. "Former hooch-mate, I want access to all the files and materials, classified or not, you have on missing Hugh Grimes. He can't be as squeaky clean as everyone says."

Chief Rogers began guffawing. "That's hilarious! Now why are the two of you really here? A donation to the police fund, eh?"

"We're here to horse trade," Abbie said. She pointed a finger. "Your investigation of the girl at the lake is--pardon me--dead in the water without even an ID of the victim."

"Give us access to all the info just mentioned and you get the name and address of the 'Lady in Red.' No access, no name."

Rogers' laugh lines froze into a frown. "You're kidding a professional, lady. You can identify her? How?"

"We'll explain once we have full and complete access to that material. Did I mention the FBI, Homeland Security and Texas Rangers?"

The Chief lit one of his long cigars. "How do I know that you're playing square with me?"

"Once we give you her name and address, you ask for a police check at that location. What could be simpler, Chester?"

Abbie extended another finger. "We will use your data right here, in this room, you watching over our shoulder."

"Give me an hour to think about this. You ask for a lot of classified stuff that I have no right to share with folks like you."

On our way out, Abbie called over her shoulder. "Remember, Chief, no access, no name!"

Once in the driveway of 101 Lake View, I hugged her hard. "Great job, Boss! I particularly like the way you stuck your finger in the Chief's red face."

Grinning at my praise, Abbie raised her eyebrows. "What's next, after we see if Lois has recovered?"

"We can recheck the bus terminal, gas station, bank and newspaper. I'd like to speak to someone in the local retired officer chapter who is familiar with Hugh and his habits. After that, visiting the Chamber of Commerce and Rotary where he's a member, might be useful."

"We also need to visit people in the flower club, golf club and church groups." Abbie checked her hair in the SUV's pull-down mirror. "He's probably a Rotarian, maybe on the Scout council as well. Several, even all of them, may have different views on Hugh Grimes as a popular, dedicated citizen."

I agreed. "Those tidbits and perspectives may help us find Hugh and return him home and get on with our lives."

"Get on with our lives?" Abbie grasped my free hand and squeezed. "I look forward to hearing more about that topic over a quiet supper tonight, but not at 101 Lake View."

I patted her knee. "That's a date. We will talk about lots of things--private things—completely unrelated to the Grimes."

Inside the residence, they were greeted by Grace, coming out of the kitchen.

"Just the person we were looking for," Abbie exclaimed. "Got a minute?"

"Sure. Good timing! You're just in time for a light lunch with Lois. Tuna sandwich and ice tea okay?"

Both of us were hungry and we answered in unison. "Sounds great!

"Before that," Abbie hesitated. "How's Lois feeling today?"

"None better! She slept like a baby last night, just like she did in times past.

"Let me tell you, she used to go to bed at nine p.m. and not wake up until ten or eleven the next morning. Mr. Hugh often got out of their bed at eleven p.m.--go to work or someplace--and be back that morning before she woke up. He always called it his 'business brain' time.

"Her spirits are higher, too, since she had a visitor Friday. Surprised you didn't see him."

Abbie asked first. "Who was he, Grace? Friend of the family?"

She fidgeted with a dish towel "Not sure I'm supposed to tell, but he's a business type from San Antonio. Not sure what he does, but he sure raised her morale."

Abbie and I exchanged puzzled glances.

She waved at Grace. "Give us a few minutes to wash. We'll be right back for that lunch with you and Lois."

Downstairs in the breakfast nook adjacent to the dining room, Lois joined Abbie and me at a small rattan-covered table.

"Sleep well?" I began.

"Like a dream," she nodded at Grace for coffee. "How about the two of you? Were you comfortable?"

"We were away checking on our so-called careers, design for me, cattle for Bruno. Yes, we are very comfortable here in your lovely home. Thanks again for having us. Just wish we spent fewer hours in my ancient SUV."

Lois raised her coffee for a trial taste. She smiled satisfaction at Grace, standing beside her. "Just right, Grace."

"Did you find any information on Hugh's whereabouts or his condition?" Lois raised dark eyebrows. "The good old local police have yet to give me any news. What did you discover?"

"The police just allowed us to read classified files pertaining to Hugh, developed by agencies like the FBI, State Police and Texas Rangers," I shrugged. "We've not studied all of them yet, but at least the local police are cooperating to that extent. That's a big plus."

"May we ask you a few more questions, Lois? You know Hugh better than his many friends and associates from whom we're getting mixed messages."

With shaking fingers, Lois selected a cigarette.

"May I?" I ignited a kitchen match with a thumb nail and held it beneath her cigarette.

She inhaled deeply before thanking me and turning to Abbie. "Ask away, dear. I intend…no, demand…to help in any way possible. I'm even taking action myself to find answers ending this terrible dream."

That surprise remark made Abbie hesitate, and look at me.

"We talked before," Abbie continued, "about anyone disliking Hugh enough to harm him. Would you again try to think of such a person, man or woman?"

"No one!" Lois angrily punched out the cigarette. "I think my husband is highly respected here in Canyon Lake as well as throughout the Hill Country. You've seen his little office downtown and talked to many of his business, church and civic associates. Didn't they all speak highly of my husband's efforts to enrich our small community?"

I nodded. "Yes, everyone we spoke to seemed impressed by Hugh's dedication. But someone, somewhere, either caused his disappearance or knows something about it."

"May I ask again," I spoke softly, "about how you knew Hugh was missing?"

"He went to town Tuesday morning to visit our bank."

"Did you see him off that morning?"

"God, no! He's a night--I should say--a morning owl. He's up long before me in the mornings. That morning, Tuesday, Hugh called me from the bank."

Before speaking, Abbie crossed her fingers and nodded at me. "Dear, does Hugh associate with many women in his work environment downtown? Might any of them hold a serious grudge against your husband concerning salary or benefits… or anything?"

Lois shut her eyes in frustration. A moment later she glared at Abbie and threw her coffee cup against the nearest wall, breaking it into tiny pieces.

"I am deeply offended by your implication that there may be a woman involved in my devoted husband's disappearance!"

Abbie apologized. "I am sorry, Lois, but we must consider all possibilities, even the most remote ones. We intend to find your husband, as you asked us. Please help us by being frank."

"We're on your side, Lois," I tried to ease the suddenly hostile atmosphere. "We're doing our best to help. If it appears otherwise," I took a breath, "perhaps Abbie and I should leave."

Lois' anguished cries and wails were instant. "No, no. Don't! You can't leave me!"

At this noise, Grace rushed into the nook, frowned at the two of us, and helped Lois back to her room.

THIRTEEN

CANYON LAKE

SATURDAY

Abbie and I sat stunned, leaning on each other in support. My phone rang, snapping us back to alertness.

"Hello," I answered. "Yes, I'm the person who put out those posters on the missing man. Do you know Mr. Grimes? Have you information about him and where he is?"

Abbie leaned forward against my ear so she could hear the answers.

"No, I don't know him. But I know his sports car, that little red one."

"Your name, sir?"

"I'm Ralph Gomez from San Marcos. We belong to the same sports car club. 'Sports Cars of the Hills,' we call ourselves. Meets monthly," he added a touch of authenticity to his report.

"Thank you, Mr. Gomez. What can you tell me about Mr. Grimes?"

"As I just said," Gomez seemed hurried to get to the reward. "Don't know him personally but I'd know that jazzy little car of his anywhere."

"Have you seen him or his car lately?"

"Sure, I did. That's why I'm calling you about that reward. Is it still available?"

"Yes, Mr. Gomez, the reward is still there for accurate information leading to the return of Mr. Grimes. That's the criteria for the reward."

"What if I just told you where I saw that little red car?"

I signaled to Abbie to take a note. "As I said, if your information leads to Mr. Grimes' return, you qualify for the reward."

"Well, I saw his car early Tuesday morning on that unnumbered one-way trail on the north side of Canyon Lake. He was going pretty fast and heading for the lake. Is that enough for my reward?"

"What time did you see him on Tuesday morning, Mr. Gomez?"

Gomez paused. "Must have been a bit after midnight. I thought it funny that he'd be out running around north of the lake at that hour.

Sports cars need good care and handling, just like a good horse, ya' know."

"Please give me your phone number and address so I can contact you later, Mr. Gomez."

Reciting phone number and address, Gomez mumbled. "Do I get the reward or not?"

"Perhaps, once we've assembled all the information, including yours. Thank you for your report, Mr. Gomez."

Abbie stood, excited. "That's great news! At least we know when he was seen at the lake! What could he have been doing there at that late hour?"

"I didn't know Hugh belonged to a sports car club. Lois never mentioned it, did she?"

"Never, partner. Maybe we're getting somewhere after all! It's been almost a week since she told us Hugh was missing. Plan to share that with your police chief buddy?"

I stared into Abbie's baby blues for a full minute. "Think Hugh is still alive, Boss?"

FOURTEEN

SAN ANTONIO

SATURDAY

That morning the Drake Investigative Service on Commerce Street was as active as a major political party convention. Several off-duty personnel, having delivered criminal lists available from the Center for Public Information all morning, sat enjoying coffee and snacks on the balcony of the building.

A parade was forming further down Commerce Street with banners and bands. The entire San Antonio Boosters Club assembled on the sidewalks, passing out leaflets asking for photos of booster activities and participants. Downtown, newspaper files were being scrutinized for photos of area politicians at social events. Prizes were being rewarded for photos of local personages attending conventions and celebrations in the Alamo City. A premium was placed on photos from political and convention parties, particularly those in hotels, bars, night clubs and restaurants.

Several Drake employees sat in a back room, reviewing patron lists purchased from San Antonio escort services.

In his office on the top floor, Don Drake, owner, was being briefed on the current collection effort by Clive, his hard-working, sometime all-night, deputy.

"That's the extent of our efforts, sir. We're off to a good start, don't you think?"

Drake opened a fresh pack of cigarettes, extracted and lighted one. "Good so far. You did yeoman work getting all this organized and started last night. There is one more thing--as the saying goes--which I think should speed our search for female acquaintances of the missing Mr. Grimes."

Always formal with his boss, Clive asked. "What's that, Mr. Drake?"

"Money, money, money, that's what!" Drake laughed and cracked his knuckles.

"Let's find a current photo of Grimes and put out a flyer to all the girls working those escort services. There must be plenty of them. One or more may remember Grimes, even tell us who were his favorite 'dates.' It's our first step in finding Grimes and getting a very big check from his wife.

"Compose a flyer, words to the effect: reward available for accurate information about the whereabouts of this client."

"I'm on it, Mr. Drake. Distribution of the flyer may be a problem, but we'll solve it!"

"Great, Clive. On with it! Brief me when you're ready for publication of the flyer. Remember, the wording has to be just right!"

FIFTEEN

CANYON LAKE

SATURDAY

Abbie and Bruno sat in the downtown Arby's, having gyros and coffee. "We've got to get busy this morning to cover all our new contacts," she passed him a napkin for a coffee spill.

He wiped his mouth. "I know and suggest we start with someone who knows Hugh pretty well. His name is Herb Glasser. Don't remember how his name popped up, but he's in that retired officer group. From my experience, those guys are all pretty chummy as well as talkative."

She grabbed the check and stood. "Then let's get an address and haul over there and talk to Mr. Herb Glasser. Then we can go to the Chamber of Commerce and ask them about Hugh."

With that they remounted the SUV and followed its directions to the Glasser address on Willow Street.

Glasser sat on a cane-bottomed chair on the front porch of an ancient red-brick cottage covered with oleanders, shrubs and flowers. He looked up at us, set an empty coffee cup on a spindly magazine table and stood.

“Hello. May I help you?” He appeared pleasant, undisturbed by two strangers standing on his porch.

“Mr. Glasser?”

“Guilty as charged,” he answered. “Is this about my taxes?”

We chuckled. “Not at all, Mr. Glasser,” Abbie grinned, trying not to laugh. ”My name is Brown and this gentleman is Bruno Carter, ex-Army, like you.”

“We'd like to talk to you about another member of the local retired officer chapter, Hugh Grimes,” I began.

“How'd you know I used to be in the Army, Mr. Carter?”

“That tattoo of the parachute badge on your upper arm gave you away, Mr. Glasser. Please call me Bruno.”

“All the way!” Glasser yelled an airborne greeting. Taken aback, Abbie jumped at the sound and grabbed my arm.

"I apologize for that," Glasser said. "It brings back old memories. Please sit down," he indicated nearby chairs.

"Now what's on your minds, lovely young lady and old airborne soldier?"

Abbie took the lead. "We're here looking for the missing husband of my old college roommate…"

"Hugh Grimes, husband of Lois," Glasser finished her sentence. "Call me Herb, folks."

"Please share with us any information you have about Hugh that might help us find him. Where do you think he might be?"

"And, why?" I added.

"Everyone's asking the same questions," Glasser mused. "He seems to be a level-headed individual with a few personal eccentricities that we all have."

Abbie nodded, taking out her notebook. "Please tell us of those and any habits you have noticed. You've known Hugh a long time?"

"I been here at the lake since retirement from the Army in '83. Guess I've known Hugh Grimes ever since. We belong to the retired officer bunch. Our chapter meets every month to tell tales, some of them a bit exaggerated, as you might guess," he cackled. "Sometimes there's even a bit of chapter business to discuss."

I began. "Did you golf or play tennis with him? Tell us about his likes and dislikes."

"That's easy," Glasser stopped. "Say, how about a cup of G.I. coffee made by an old G.I.?"

I followed Herb into a small, spotless kitchen and carried three cups to a porch table. Herb brought out a blackened coffee pot and filled the cups.

"Your health!" he proposed. "If my coffee can't kill you, nothing will!"

We grinned and clinked cups.

"Well, back to Hugh," he began. "He loves to talk about his service in Germany and Viet Nam.

"Been there, Bruno?"

"Yes, sir, both places."

"I'm off the subject again, aren't I? He loves that little red sports car, always tinkering with it, always taking it to the garage to get fixed what he'd just repaired. Aside from the car, he really liked fishing.

"He claimed several prizes for the biggest bass or catfish caught in our lake. I fished with him several times but we never caught much. Said he had a favorite fishing spot but never took me there."

"Did the two of you take any lady friends fishing?"

"Bruno! You know lovin' and fishin' don't mix!"

"Your coffee's a bit strong, but tasty," Abbie quipped, replacing her cup on the table. "Did you and he meet any ladies at those retired officer get-togethers?"

"Naw, we were both straight arrow."

I scratched my head, searching for another question. “Know anyone who disliked Hugh enough to harm him or his reputation?”

“No. Everyone I know thinks highly of Hugh… and his missus as well.”

Abbie shrugged. Apparently, like me, she also was out of questions.

I stood and carried the cups back to the kitchen. “Nice meeting you, Herb. If we may, we might be back if we have more questions.”

“Thanks for that excellent cup of coffee, Herb,” Abbie said.

“Coffee’s always hot. Come by anytime! We’ll tell some wild jump stories, Bruno, like tangled canopies and tall tree landings!”

The sun had raised the temperature inside our closed SUV to boil/bake. We hurriedly rolled down the windows to cool off.

Abbie asked, “Did we gain anything startling there?” She opened her notebook as we started toward town and the Chamber of Commerce.

She looked up from her notes, puzzled. “What’s a straight arrow?”

“A straight arrow is someone who obeys all the scout laws.”

“Huh?”

"You know: trustworthy, loyal, helpful, friendly, courteous, kind, obedient, cheerful, thrifty, brave, clean and reverent." I took a deep breath.

She punched me in the ribs. "You mean you were all those things?"

"Yes, dear Boss."

"I intend to examine you privately for your next merit badge. I'll test you for all those attributes, so, be prepared."

"Did you know that's the scout motto?" I blurted. "Be Prepared. I'm ready and eager for examination, scout master."

The chamber of commerce was in a one-story white brick building, once home to a bank. We walked in and asked for the event coordinator.

A young woman dressed in tight jeans, western shirt and big hat approached us in the visitor area.

"Howdy, I'm Vicki. We're all dressed up today for the big livestock sale, rodeo and dance tonight. I hope you two can come?"

"Howdy, yourself," I answered in kind. "We're Abbie and Bruno."

Abbie looked at me before answering. "Have to check our schedule," she waffled. "We're here to ask about the town's missing man, Hugh Grimes, a member of your board of directors. Have you heard from Hugh lately? We're trying to locate him for his wife."

"Ah, yes, poor Lois. Please give her our best. This must be a very trying period for her, not knowing his whereabouts."

Vicki studied us for a moment. "No, I haven't heard a thing. Being a director, he's usually here working several hours each week.

"Hugh was a previous organizer of our stock show and rodeo. We really could use him here and now. Have you discovered anything about where he might be?"

"No, that's why we came, hoping you might have some news of him."

Vicki pushed the big cowboy hat back off her forehead. "Our board meets this afternoon, prior to the big show at the stock yards. I'll be happy to ask if they've heard anything about Hugh."

She looked dubious as I handed her my card with cell phone number. "Please let us know anything you find at the board meeting. Perhaps we'll catch up with you at the rodeo tonight."

This seemed to cheer her. "Better come before six o'clock since parking is limited. I'll look for you two. Don't forget the dance at eight!"

"Oh, Vicki," I paused at the door. "Could we rent an exhibit spot at the stock show tonight? We need one with a big black board for notices?"

Absently, she studied the card I'd just given her. "Sure. What do you intend to exhibit?"

Abbie looked as puzzled as Vicki.

I looked at Abbie. "We still have all those extra posters with Hugh's photo on them, don't we?"

Abbie beamed. "Great idea! We'll post them in our booth at the stock show and hope someone sees Hugh's photo and remembers where and when they saw him!"

"Bingo!" I yelled, adding to Vicki's confusion.

After tacking the extra posters with Hugh's photo on the borrowed bulletin board in our newly rented booth, we sat waiting for reactions that night. Lots of family groups stopped to look at the posters and discuss the offer of a reward. Most read aloud our words on the poster:

HELP US FIND MISSING BUSINESSMAN
HUGH GRIMES, AGE 55, OF CANYON LAKE
$500 REWARD IS OFFERED FOR INFO
LEADING TO FINDING GRIMES

Comments from those studying the posters ranged from "I think I saw him in the Fourth of July Parade," or "Wasn't he our mayor a couple of years ago?"

We stood by with notebooks at the ready, anxious to capture any leads to Hugh's location.

A sunburned rancher studied Hugh's photo, pointed to the judging area. "I saw him! He was judging Brangus steers right over there..."

I jumped over the table and began running toward the judging area.

"Whoa, whoa," the rancher yelled. "I meant I seen him there last fall. Do I still get that reward?"

I answered firmly. "No, sir. No current information, no reward."

Disappointed and shaking his head, the man stopped at the nearest tent selling cold beer to ease his loss.

I frowned at Abbie, who grinned and gave me a thumbs-up. "Hang in there, cowboy. We're bound to get some good clues soon!"

A florid middle-aged man in overalls studied Grimes' photo. He turned to Abbie. "Believe I saw that man fishing on the north side of the lake last month. Sure looked like him," he touched the photo.

Abbie reacted. "Remember exactly where you saw him and when?"

The man pursed his lips and spit tobacco juice. "'Scuse me. No, Ma'm. I can't recall exactly where he was, but I saw him land a great big ole bass."

"Can you recall when you saw him?"

"Well, the season had just opened, but I can't be specific on the exact date. Sorry."

Near midnight we decided to vacate our rented booth, recover the posters and head home. On the way to 101 Lake View, we stopped and treated ourselves to cold beer and brisket sandwiches.

"Best move we've made all day, partner," Abbie yawned and put her arm around me as we drove home.

SIXTEEN

SAN ANTONIO

SUNDAY

Clive knocked gingerly on Drake's partially open office door at eight a.m. He carried a revised copy of the announcement he'd worked on since midnight. It was a plea to escort hostesses to provide information on a client they might remember named Hugh Grimes of Canyon Lake.

Earlier, Clive rubbed his aching eyes and mused aloud at midnight Saturday "How do I start this letter to girls working as escorts? My letter must encourage them to volunteer client information. I bet that's a subject they never discuss with anyone."

He had a smoke and began another draft on his laptop.

"Dear Ms. ______

Please answer the following:

Question 1. Do you now or have you ever entertained a businessman/client named Hugh Grimes? (see his photo, below)

Question 2. Do you know any other escort/hostess who may be familiar with this client?

If your answer to either of the above questions is yes, you are eligible for a sizable reward, presuming your information helps us locate this client.

Your responses to these questions will not be shared with any agency or any person other than your own personal interviewer. This is a private, confidential matter not to be discussed with anyone other than at the time and place convenient for your personal, confidential interview. Please call 800-357-5937 at any hour to schedule your individual, personal and private interview. Thank you.

The more useful your information, the better your chances of winning a reward valued at $3,000 to $5,000!"

"Maybe not a literary prize winner," Clive said aloud. "But it's the best I can do on short notice."

He entered Drake's office with his draft in hand. "Good morning, Mr. Drake."

"Hello, Clive. Got that announcement, have you? Let's see it."

In silence, Drake read the draft several times.

"Well done, Clive! Sounds like a winner to me! Think there will be many ayes to your questions?"

"Hopefully, Mr. Drake, we'll get ayes by the dozen. We even have extra telephone operators available to take all the calls."

Drake looked at the draft again. "Who is going to be our 'personal and private' interviewer?"

"I selected two motherly-sounding females to handle the interviews and transcribe the names."

"Okay, Clive. Put the show on the road and keep me advised. Right?"

"Right, Mr. Drake!"

SEVENTEEN

CANYON LAKE

MONDAY

Abbie looked sharply at me. “Out with it! You seem unhappy about something this morning. What is it?”

I shook my head. “Local law enforcement is what! It seems to be doing nothing about our prominent local businessman, missing for almost a week now.

“What can we tell Lois about her missing husband? We don’t even know if Hugh is alive or not. Damn the police!”

“Calm down, Bruno! Let’s off to see your friend, Police Chief Chester Rogers, in his lair.”

“I’m also disappointed,” I made a face, “that we lack a good lead about Lois’ missing husband. And he's been missing for a week tomorrow! What do we tell her after enjoying her hospitality all week?"

"C'mon, grouch. Maybe we'll get a clue at the police."

At the police station downtown, we entered in step, seeking answers.

"We're here to see the Chief," Abbie took the lead, "about that local man who's been missing almost a week."

The tone of her voice caused everyone in the office to freeze. The Chief's door opened immediately.

"Well, who do we have here?" he grinned. "Are you two citizens still helping Mrs. Grimes find her husband? Have you found him? Is he here? Where is he?"

"Chester," I spoke the word loudly so the whole station could hear, "we need an update on the Grimes case. Don't you have any new information about him? He's been missing a week."

"Come in, come in," Rogers backtracked and closed the door behind us. He remained standing behind his desk without offering us chairs.

"Is your investigator on another case, Chester? We already provided you the identity of the drowned girl. Was it homicide or accident? Have you made any arrests yet?"

Rogers' face became redder with each question. He took a breath and doubled his fists. "Friend or not, you're obstructing law enforcement efforts. I should arrest you! Now get out of here fast, both of you, or I will!"

"Calm down, calm down," I repeated Abbie's earlier words. "Look, Chester. You owe Mrs. Grimes an update on her husband's case. Have you any leads where he is…or his sports car? What can we tell her?"

Exasperated, Rogers held up his hands. "Tell her we're working hard to find her husband. Like you, we've been to the gas station, bus station, bank… everywhere."

"Yeah, your investigator's been following us around all those places," I said. "Had he come to us first, we could have saved him lots of time."

Rogers opened his door and pointed. "Get out of here!"

I couldn't resist a parting shot. "You coming up for reelection soon, Chester? Good luck with that!"

We drove up to 101 Lake View and parked our grimy SUV beside Lois' shiny new Lexus ES sedan. I made a mental note for a wash and oil change the next morning. As usual, Grace had the door open before we climbed all the steps.

"Shhhh," she cautioned. "Mrs. Grimes is in bed and not feeling well."

"What happened?" Abbie frowned.

"Don't know but it has something to do with that man from San Antonio. He called her today."

"The one who was here Friday? You said his visit made her happy."

Grace nodded. "I remember, but whatever he told her today must have been mighty bad."

Abbie reflected. "Did he leave a business card, Grace?"

"Yes, he did. He told me to be sure and call him if Lois needed medical attention. Just a minute and I'll look in the pantry for that little card of his."

Minutes later, Grace was back, proudly holding an elaborate calling card. Abbie took it and read aloud:

> Mr. Donald Drake, President
> Drake Investigative Services
> 800-245- 3486
> 1128 Highway 281
> San Antonio, TX 78943

"Uh oh," she passed the card to me. "She has hired an investigator to look for Hugh."

I studied the card, took its picture with my phone, and returned the card to Grace.

"His call today must have been bad news. If Drake had found Hugh alive, Lois would be happy."

Abbie drew a deep breath. "Since Lois is ill and in bed, Drake may have told her that Hugh is dead..."

I interrupted. "Or perhaps Hugh has run away and Drake located him in Mexico or somewhere?"

"That's crazy," Abbie shook her head. "We'll just have to ask Lois when she's better."

I offered another idea. "Instead, let's ask Drake what he told her."

"No, that won't work. Lois is his client. He can't ethically give us any information."

"Who says he's ethical?" I argued. "We explain we're here to help Lois find Hugh."

Abbie countered. "Okay, how about just telephoning Drake, instead of visiting?"

"He's less likely to tell us anything without seeing us in person," I reasoned.

"Okay, on to San Antonio! I need to check-in at my office there anyway."

EIGHTEEN

CANYON LAKE

MONDAY

We were on our way to San Antonio via Highway 281 when we heard the high whine of a patrol car catching up, and sitting on our SUV's back bumper.

"Better pull over and see what they want." Abbie turned around to look at the black and white police sedan.

"It's marked 'Canyon Lake Police."

"Guess who sent them after us?" I growled. "We were only going fifty-five in a sixty zone."

The police car loudspeaker came on, loud.

"Stop your vehicle and turn off the engine!"

The next command was "Both of you, place your hands on the dashboard in plain sight!"

A deputy sheriff was at my window, his holster strap unbuckled, peering first at us, then at the empty back seat.

"Driver's license and proof of insurance, sir."

Deftly, Abbie opened the glove compartment and handed the insurance card to me.

Unexpectedly, the deputy next ordered, "Step out of the vehicle, both of you."

"Just do it, please," Abbie urged apoplectic me.

Opening a ticket book, the deputy read aloud the notes he was making.

"Back license plate is hanging by a single screw. You were going sixty-one miles an hour in a sixty zone. And…"

The deputy looked up and smiled. "And your safety sticker expired Monday. You will have to secure your vehicle, sir, and come with me."

Once Abbie and I, both steaming, were out of the SUV, we had to cram into the crowded back seat of the patrol car.

We both asked, "Where are we going?"

The deputy smiled and said, "You are being returned to Canyon Lake for examination and booking on the charges just read to you."

Were it not for Abbie holding both my hands, I might have resisted. "Calm down, dear," she urged. "This won't take long. Then we'll be on our way," she whispered.

Abbie continued patting my hand as we endured the ride back to Canyon Lake, then being led into the police office, like criminals.

Inside the Chief's office, I stuck an accusing finger in his face.

"Hell of a way to treat a buddy, Chester! It's not like you to act this way! Why are you doing this? You owe me one, a great big one. Instead you have one of your troops pull us in!"

"We are private citizens on our way to San Antonio," Abbie added, not wanting to be left behind from the accusation.

Chief Rogers smacked his hand on the desk. "What is your business in San Antonio?"

We both answered, "Private business!"

"Hadn't anything to do with this?"

He read from a note. "The Drake Investigative Service? What's that?"

"Private business," I repeated, calmer now. "You've had your fun, Chester. Can we go about our private business now?"

"Sit down, sit down," Rogers said, activating his intercom. "Doris, could we have some coffee in here, please? Three cups."

"Now," Rogers smiled at last. "Tell me about this Drake Investigative Service."

I looked at Abbie. She nodded.

"First, tell us about the 'Lady in Red' we identified for you."

Rogers glanced at a report. "Thanks for your assistance, but the investigator would have eventually identified her anyway."

I leaned forward, balancing a hot cup of coffee in my lap. "Her name?"

"Bernice Stone," Rogers read. "She recently moved to Dallas, no others listed at her Dallas address on Throckmorton Street. No bank account according to Dallas Police."

"Previous residence?"

"Ask the Dallas police," Rogers said dryly. "They have listed her as missing. Now tell me about this Drake business."

Abbie sat straighter. "First, tell us how Bernice Stone, wearing only red panties and matching bra, got to town, then into the lake."

"We're checking on that." Rogers said flatly.

"You need a better investigator," I smiled. "He didn't gather much information on the late Ms. Stone. Do you know if she was married, had children, other relatives, where she worked or anything?"

Rogers stared at me. "We have asked for more information, but nothing received as yet. You're quibbling! Tell me about Drake!"

Abbie nudged me and answered. “Okay. We think that Drake has been privately hired by Mrs. Grimes to investigate her husband’s disappearance. Can you blame her since you haven’t learned anything about him, his condition or location since Tuesday?”

“Halt right there!” Rogers stood up, red-faced. “Why didn’t you tell me she had hired a private investigator?”

“We didn’t know about it until this morning!” I stood, replying in kind. “It looks like Drake telephoned Mrs. Grimes last night with some news about Hugh.

“Whatever he told her must have been very bad, since she’s been in bed since their conversation, according to Lois’ companion.”

“You two were on your way to San Antonio, weren’t you?” It was Roger’s time to poke a finger in my face.

“You wanted to know what he’d discovered that so upset your client, right? You two are out of a job, if he found the husband is dead, eh?

“Even PI’s have rules and regulations, Bruno, just like the Army. Sure, you can go see him, but he won’t tell you squat.”

I took a deep breath. “Why don’t you, Police Chief of Canyon Lake, ask Drake in your official capacity what he's come up with about her missing husband?"

"Nix!" Rogers resounded immediately. "A PI will reveal his results only to the client. Otherwise, he loses his license and there goes his fancy livelihood!"

Abbie and Bruno looked at each other. "What is your reason for our arrest, Chief?"

Rogers sat down heavily and motioned toward the door. "You were not arrested, just brought in for questioning concerning the murder of that young woman at Canyon Lake.

"I am warning you two, I'll arrest you in a heart beat if you withhold any information. If you two amateurs learn anything from Drake, you'd damn better share it with me!

Meanwhile," he snickered. "I'll have adjoining cells readied with clean sheets awaiting your return."

NINETEEN

ENROUTE TO SAN ANTONIO

MONDAY

We stopped at the Texaco station to gas up for our trip. "Hi, Ted," I waved and he came over to our pump.

"Fill 'er up?" he asked.

"Please. By the way, Ted, any news about the missing Mr. Grimes?"

"'Nary a peep," he replied.

"Haven't seen his little red sports car, have you?"

"No, and don't want to, either. I bet he's no longer with us."

"Who said that?"

"Just figures. If no one's seen him eatin', drinkin' or sleepin,' he must have died."

"Still have my card, Ted?"

"Sure do, Mr. Bruno. And if I see Mr. Grimes or hear about him, I'll be sure to let you know."

Abbie pressed my hand as I started the SUV. "Before we get off to San Antonio, let's go by 101 Lake View and see if Lois is any better."

"Good idea, Boss. Maybe she'll tell us--more likely, you--what's wrong."

She pinched my ear. "What's wrong is your keep calling me Boss."

"Yes, dear," I responded. "No more 'Boss,' just 'Yes, Dear.' How's that?"

"Much better." she kissed the pinched spot.

As always, Grace met us at the door of 101 Lake View before we reached it.

"How's Lois, Grace?"

"'Bout the same, but she did eat a little breakfast a while ago."

"Think she'd mind seeing Bruno and me?"

"I just don't know about her, since that San Antonio man called. She cries a lot and seems more moody than usual. Maybe you could brighten her day."

"Has her doctor been here?"

"Yes, M'am. He called it depression, but didn't leave a prescription so I guess she's not so bad."

After Grace announced her, Abbie entered Lois' bedroom. I waited in the hall.

Later, on our way out of town, Abbie relaxed and described Lois. "She looks normal but a little pale. She asked about you…no… about us. I lied and told her we were wonderful."

"How's that a lie?" I asked. "I think we are a wonderful…couple." I managed the last word easily.

"Me, too," she patted my cheek. "Back to Lois, she said she was feeling wacky--as she called it--since the phone call from that man in San Antonio named Drake. He told her. Hugh had been seen with several women in and around San Antonio the last several months. He wouldn't tell her who or where, but said the women were 'pick-ups,' as he called them.

Abbie faced me to describe Lois' reaction.

"God!" she said, "Lois exploded! How could I have been so damned dumb? I wasn't even aware of his frequent out-of-town 'business conferences' as he called them.

"Dumb, dumb, dumb!" Lois repeated, slapping her forehead.

"That's terrible," I blinked, not knowing what else to say. "Does Drake know where Hugh is?"

"He told her he is still searching, but didn't know Hugh's location yet."

Thinking, I rubbed my forehead. "At least, Hugh is alive somewhere."

"At the moment, Lois doesn't seem to care. She's considering divorce as soon as he's found."

"If he is found!" I pulled the SUV to the side of the road and put my arms around Abbie. "Let's don't let their ending spoil what we're just beginning."

She looked at me, big blues watchful.

I spent several minutes reassuring her, then I pulled back onto the highway and we speeded to her place on San Pedro.

TWENTY

SAN ANTONIO

MONDAY P.M.

Don Drake pushed his chair back and lit a cigarette with one hand while shuffling color photos on a cluttered desk. Clive, his deputy, nervously paced beside the desk.

"Jeez! You got a great response from that flyer we published. Did it go to all escort services?"

"All of those in the phone book, Mr. Drake."

"The girls don't all expect money, do they?"

"No, sir. We are very careful in explaining the rules for the reward."

Drake rubbed his hands gleefully. "Some of these girls are beautiful, Clive! No wonder business men like our good old Hugh Grimes falls for them."

"The trick for us, Mr. Drake, is locating the ones who claim to 'know' Grimes. Then locate and interview each one. Where did they see him last? Who are his favorites? What are his favorite bars and haunts?"

Drake rubbed his hands together. "Then go after him and find him!"

He paused, amused. "Am I missing anything, Clive?"

"Yes, sir! You left out presenting our big bill to the wife and a reminder that she promised you a big bonus for his discovery.

"What if we find the guy is dead, Mr. Drake?"

"She still gets the bill," Drake grinned, "with our sincerest condolences, of course. Now get out there and speed up those interviews."

"Hello, is Miss Gaylord there please?"

"Yeah, this is me right here. Are you calling for a date?"

"No, Miss Gaylord. You answered a recent flyer concerning a search for a client named Hugh. Remember?"

"What I remember best (coughing interrupts the words) is that promised reward of between three and five thou. Ask away."

"Do you know Hugh Grimes?"

"Sure, sure. When do I get the reward?"

"First, your information must help us locate Mr. Grimes. Nothing is automatic and your information must be accurate in all respects for you to be eligible."

"Yeah, yeah, I hear you. My information is just as accurate as one of them NASA moon rockets."

"Where and when did you last see this client?"

"At the Chicken Shack on 12th Street. Know it?"

"What were you doing there?"

"Having a snack before a quick backseat job in a Jeep. Cramped! You know what I mean?"

"Know any other working girls who know this client?"

"Honey, if I did, I'm not sharing the reward with nobody. Now, when do I get the money?"

"We have your mailing address, Miss Gaylord. If you are the winner after all the information is collected and compared. you will receive a check in the mail."

"Check in the mail, huh? I've heard that one before. If I don't get my money, I'm sending some friends to collect from you.

"Hey, what's your name, mister?"

"Hello, I'm looking for Miss Sharon Neighbors."

"You found me, buddy. What can I do for you? Or… to get down to brass tacks, what can you do me for? You need a personal and private date? If the answer is yes, you just hit a home run!"

"No. I'm not looking for a date, Miss Neighbors. You responded to a recent flyer about our search for a client named Hugh Grimes. Remember the flyer?"

"Sure, I remember it. It was so long, it caused my pen to run dry. Too long!"

"Miss Neighbors, do you recall a client named Hugh Grimes?"

"We don't go by names, mister. What does this guy look like?"

"Grimes is a successful businessman from a little town north of San Antonio named Canyon Lake. He's about five feet, nine inches tall, weighs 180. Has black hair turning grey and drives a little red sports car."

"Hey, I remember that red sports car. He took me for a spin in it. Later, I took him for a spin. Know what I mean?

"Was this the flyer about a reward for info concerning this Grimes guy? I'm in! Sign me up for the reward!"

"To qualify for a reward, Miss, you have to provide true answers to the following."

"Okay, shoot me the questions,"

"Where did you meet Grimes? Was it in San Antonio or elsewhere?"

"Right there in the good old Alamo City, at that big bar at Goliad and Yerks. He bought me five dollar drinks all night. At least until I got him comfortable elsewhere."

"Thank you, Miss. Do you know any other hostesses who may be familiar with Mr. Grimes?"

"What kind of dumb question is that? No! Ladies don't share information like that!

"Time for me to ask you a question, buddy. When do I get my money?"

"Hello, I'm looking or Miss Margaret Bond. Is that you?"

"Sure is, Mister. I'm Peggy. Margaret is my stage name. I'm often featured in playhouse productions throughout South Texas. Maybe you've seen me in one of them? Like 'Margaret Bond in the Bubble Bath Boudoir?"

"No, Miss. I haven't had the pleasure. You completed a recent survey we sent you concerning a client named Grimes. Do you remember the survey?"

"Yeah, before I opened it, I was afraid it was something from the IRS."

"Did you complete the survey?"

"Sure did, and I'm excited about that reward mentioned in it. When do I get it?"

"Answer a few more questions for me, Miss. Do you know a client named Hugh Grimes?"

"Yeah, I may know him. Is he that big spender with the little red sports car?"

"Right you are, Miss! With a memory like yours, I bet you remember where you met Mr. Grimes?"

"If I answer this one, do I get the prize money?"

"The money will be awarded once all responses, like yours, are graded. Your answers must be accurate to be considered for a reward. Where did you and Grimes meet?"

"Let me think. It was the Fourth of July and we were celebrating at that fancy upstairs bar in the Hilton."

"Miss, do you know another hostess who is acquainted with Grimes?"

"And allow her to compete with me for the bonus? Get lost!"

"Thank you for your responses, Miss. If you win, you will receive a letter from us declaring you the winner of the grand prize!"

"Hooray!"

Clive was briefing Mr. Drake on a few of the interviews resulting from the flyers mailed to all escort hostesses in San Antonio.

"Here is a sample of our interviews of three escort hostesses. Most of the interviews identify bars, restaurants, and hotels where Grimes recently has been entertained by hostesses.

"Now, we take a photo of Grimes and look for him at these specific places until we find him. All that remains is to complete a detailed bill of our services and present it to our wealthy client, Mrs. Grimes.

"Case closed!"

TWENTY ONE

CANYON LAKE

TUESDAY

Chief Rogers was having a tough morning. His coffee turned cold as he stared at another red-bordered headline on the morning newspaper.

"Get that newspaper editor on the phone for me, Betty. Plus a hot cup of coffee, please."

Silently, Rogers fumed as he reread the headline.

CASE OF SLAIN 'LADY IN RED' STILL
UNSOLVED AFTER ONE WEEK
POLICE ASK FOR HELP

"The editor is on the line, Chief," Betty whispered as she set a cup of coffee on the corner of his desk.

"This is Reese Turner. What can the *Canyon Lake Caller* do for you today, Chief?"

"You starting a 'Defund the Police' movement in Canyon Lake because Rose, your hotshot reporter, isn't getting as many press releases from the police as she likes? What's your motive, Reese, in defaming your local law and order police?

"Dammit! We're working day and night on your so-called 'Lady in Red' case. First, we were able to identify the body without help from county or state. Now we're working non-stop to find out what happened to her!

"Not a single witness, remember! No signs of struggle on the body, remember?

"What the hell do you and your frilly female reporter expect of us, other than continue to dig for answers? We're not happy with our progress, either. Our small staff and budget, which were recently cut--thank you for that terrible editorial--are working day and night on this case.

"I'd appreciate your retraction of today's New York-style headline and an acknowledgment that your police are working 16 hour shifts to solve this case!"

Chief Rogers slammed down the phone and grabbed his coffee cup. After draining it, he was calmer and asked Deputy Lorrance and Investigator Francis to update him on the case at eleven o'clock.

At 101 Lake View Drive, Abbie and I were having coffee, discussing whether we should telephone Don Drake in San Antonio.

“We’ve never even met the guy,” Abbie argued. “He’ll cite client confidentiality and hang up on us as soon as we mention Lois.”

I countered. “At least he could tell us the bad news that’s given bedridden Lois a bad case of depression.”

“Should, could,” Abbie mocked me. “He doesn’t care that we are here to help Lois find her husband. Why should he share anything that might be useful to us?”

Once she finished her coffee, I handed Abbie a homemade margarita, made from Lois’ recipe. Despite the early hour, I wanted to ease the tension in Abbie’s face.

“Tell you what,” I said after she downed the trial margarita. “I’ll pay for the call. You can even listen, to make sure I don’t over commit us.”

The Drake Investigative Service number from the card given to Gwen answered immediately. I took a deep breath.

“My name is Carter, a friend of Mrs. Lois Grimes, a client of your services. May I speak to Mr. Drake about Mrs. Grime’s medical condition since his report to her last Friday?”

I was as surprised as Abbie when Drake came to the phone minutes later. Another deep breath. Abbie listened in, ear to the phone.

"Hello, Mr. Drake. I'm Bruno Carter. My partner, Ms. Abbie Brown, and I have been attempting to aid Mrs. Lois Grimes of Canyon Lake find her husband. Lois asked us to stay with her temporarily until Hugh's return.

"Mrs. Grimes' companion told us after your call Friday, that Mrs. Grimes acted unusually depressed, even refusing to speak to her."

"Sorry to hear that, Mr....Carter," Drake said. "How may I help?"

Hearing Drake's words, Abbie stood and silently cheered.

"We thought we might improve Lois' depression if we knew what you told her that apparently frightened her. We realize this is an unusual request.

"Our purpose is to aid Lois through this very difficult period until her husband returns. Any information you can share with us will not be divulged to anyone but Lois."

It was several minutes before Drake responded.

"I can tell you that my verbal report covered her husband's activities in the San Antonio area. I sincerely regret telling her our findings since they apparently depressed her. At the time, I thought she was considering filing for a divorce based upon our evidence."

Abbie raised her eyebrows at the mention of divorce.

"Thank you for that explanation, Mr. Drake." I hesitated. "Have you been able to locate Mr. Grimes?"

"Not as yet. I'm unsure if Mrs. Grimes wants us to continue our search. If it won't upset her, perhaps I should ask her if we should stop our investigation of his whereabouts."

"Thanks for the information, Mr. Drake. Based on what you just said about the possibility of divorce, I don't know how Lois might answer your question about discontinuing the search."

Abbie rose to leave, and paused. "Won't hurt to ask her, Mr. Drake. She'll need Hugh's present address for the divorce papers."

Chief Roger's telephone rang again. "Oh, Lord," he supported his forehead with one hand while picking up the instrument with the other. "Please, not another call about that blasted headline!"

This time the caller was Doctor Mills, the medical examiner.

"Hi, Chief. Just thought you ought to know we may have a homicide instead of an accidental drowning on our hands."

Rogers grabbed his notebook. "You mean the body at the lake, the 'Lady in Red"?

"'Fraid so. I examined the body again, once most of the water had seeped, and found something very peculiar."

"What?"

"There are ligatures on the ankles. They could have been caused by something binding the ankles together, like a rope. The ligatures might be rope burns. I'll further examine them microscopically, of course.

"Chief, can you start a search of the lake and beach for a rope, probably a long one of about one inch in diameter?"

Doctor Mills wiped his forehead with his sleeve. "I can't imagine why anyone would rope her legs together. Can you?

"The marks weren't visible earlier, but they are now since the moisture has abated. Based on this, I am obliged to change my finding from accident to homicide.

"Thought I'd better give you a heads-up before Rose, that reporter, somehow gets wind of this. It'll be another red-lined headline in the newspaper!"

Rogers erupted. "Don't you dare call her, hear? Mum's the word! Don't tell anybody!"

"I won't, Chief, but the truth will eventually come out. You know that."

"Yeah, I know. Since it's now a homicide, Texas Rangers--maybe FBI--will take over this case. I'm calling them right now."

Rogers slumped in his chair, wishing his cup contained bourbon instead of Betty's coffee.

TWENTY TWO

SAN ANTONIO

WEDNESDAY

Clive was so jubilant he forgot to knock before entering Drake's office.

"Bonanza, Boss!"

"I need some good news. Tell me!" Drake looked up, grinning expectantly.

"We found a new group of gents, called the Wanderers, to which Hugh Grimes belongs. It's right here in San Antonio!"

"Wanderers? Never heard of them."

Clive held out an information sheet. "They used to be called the Martini Club. It's a small bunch of rich business men who enjoy a good time."

"And?"

"The Wanderers hosted a small, by special invitation only, party for themselves last month.

One of the members had the bright idea to enliven the party. He invited all the hostesses from one of the most expensive dating clubs in town."

Drake loosened his silk tie. "I bet you located a photographer who snapped a few pictures of that happy mixture of hostesses and rich businessmen?"

Clive was ecstatic. "Yes, sir! Guess who was one of these rich businessmen?"

"If you're going to say Hugh Grimes, bingo, you deserve a raise! But how do his photos help us find the man?"

Without being asked, Clive took the chair in front of the desk. "The manager of an escort service knows his girls by heart. After all, they are his bread and butter. He knows each one. He can identify any of his girls who were photographed with Grimes."

Drake guessed aloud. "Next step, we interview the girls who may be able to tell us where Grimes likes to hide!"

"Right, Boss! It's much better than using those flyers and telephone interviews."

"Good work, Clive. Get on to it!

"By the way, Clive, I telephoned our client, Mrs. Grimes, today. I asked her if we should continue looking for her husband.

"Yes!' was her answer. She wants to look Grimes in the eye and tell him she's suing for divorce.

"What do you suppose that means for us, Clive?"

"A bigger bill for our services!"

TWENTY THREE

CANYON LAKE

WEDNESDAY

As was the custom, the meeting began by the ringing of a cow bell by the Sergeant of Arms. Standing behind a podium borrowed from the VFW, Herb Glasser, President of the Retired Officer Association, began.

"Ladies and gentlemen, this is an emergency meeting in response to that newspaper headline yesterday.

"I'm going to read the big red headline which occasioned our special meeting today."

QUOTE. Case of Slain 'Lady in Red' Still Unsolved after One Week. Police ask for help. UNQUOTE.

"We have copies of that front page article posted on all four walls of our chapter. See?" Glasser pointed out the pages on the walls.

"If you didn't read that article, please take the time to do so right now. I'm declaring a ten minute recess for your reading.

"Please get up and read it 'cause next we're going to discuss how our chapter can help the local police.

"Ten minute recess starts now," Glasser pointed at the wall clock and sat down.

Several members arose and went to the nearest wall to read the article.

At the end of the ten minutes, I stood behind the podium and resumed speaking. "First, let me introduce the newest member of our chapter, Mr. Bruno Carter, a resident of Kerrville. He's here visiting Mrs. Lois Grimes.

"Glad to have you, Bruno. He's a Vietnam veteran like many of us. Welcome, Bruno!"

I stood, waved to a smattering of applause, and sat down.

"Our police need help," Glasser said. "They are overloaded by the tragic case of that female found dead on the beach Tuesday.

"Now, we can stand by and shake our heads about that tragic death in our own backyard. Or," he emphasized the word, "we can render our police some kind of assistance.

"Do I hear a motion?" Glasser looked at the corner where his cronies sat, primed to answer.

Bob Runstadt stood in the corner, waving his hand. "Mr. President, I move that our chapter of the Retired Officer Association assist our police in some meaningful way."

"Do I hear a second?" Glasser looked to the other corner.

Someone there called out, "Second!"

"If things worked this harmoniously in Washington, we'd have a different country," a female member shouted from the center floor.

"And a much better country, too," another female voice joined her, followed by a series of 'yeahs' and applause.

Glasser hammered his gavel on the podium to regain control.

"It's been moved and seconded that our chapter aid the police in this emergency. That means that each one of us must take an active part in whatever action we decide."

Runstadt, also the parliamentarian, rose again. "I call for a vote on the motion just presented."

"Right!" Glasser used the gavel again.

"All in favor of the motion just presented and seconded, to assist the police in a manner yet to be decided, say 'yes."

The 'yes's rebounded loudly off the thin sheetrock walls, rattling the newspaper articles hanging there.

"All opposed to the motion, so signify by saying 'no."

There were only two 'no' votes cast, and those quietly.

"The motion is carried by a majority!" Glasser said, turning to the chapter secretary. "Are you taking all this down, Roger?"

"Now we come to the difficult part," murmured Richard Hawkins from the back row.

"That's right, Richard," Glasser heard him. "There's always a hard part.

"Now, let's see a show of hands of members who would like to be on a panel to discuss likely avenues of approach…I mean by that, what actions the chapter might take in support of our police.

"Don't be bashful," Glasser eyed his audience. "A show of hands, please."

One hand was raised from the center. """I'm not volunteering, Mr. President. I have a question: are these 'actions' as you call them going to cost us money?

"Speaking as our treasurer, we need funding 'cause we don't have a pile of money at our disposal right now."

"Good point, Felix. We'll seek funds from other local organizations, like the Legion and VFW, plus local businesses like the bank, churches, Rotarians, Masons, Lions, and others.

"But before we ask for donations, we must have a clear, supportable, understandable, program of actions helpful to the police. No cake and cookie sales, no dinner tickets, no yard or rummage sales. Questions?"

No hands were raised from a suddenly quiet audience.

"Again, let's see the hands of volunteers to serve on a panel to select helpful actions to support and assist law and order in our community."

The chapter secretary, Roger Folsom, stood up. "I might suggest, Mr. President, instead of raising hands, we pass around a sign-up roster."

A female stood up beside Folsom. "I like that better. I can see with whom I'll be working."

Folsom immediately stood with a clip board and started it on the front row. People began nodding and signing the clipboard being passed from person to person, row to row.

"Let's have a temporary adjournment while the clipboard is being passed around," Glasser announced.

"At our next meeting and I suggest tomorrow, same place, same time, we'll announce the names of the members who volunteered to be on our panel and get them started. This is a serious undertaking which will make us proud of our chapter's participation."

A female voice loudly repeated another's earlier declaration. "If things worked this well in Washington, we'd have a different and better county."

At the conclusion of the meeting, I made my way to Herb, standing amid well-wishers at the front. Once their conversations eventually ebbed, I took him by the arm.

"Got a minute, Herb? I've an idea about helping the police, but it needs your approval and help."

"Sure, Bruno. What's up?"

"How about we scour the beach where the body was found, in case the police overlooked something that might be significant. Only a few volunteers, a dozen or so, could search the beach area near where the body was found. Maybe someone in the chapter has a metal detector to improve the thoroughness of our search. It shouldn't take more than a few hours. I doubt the police took much time to look around, except for the area right around the 'Lady in Red's' body.

"If you want to get some recognition for our chapter, Herb, we tell *The Canyon Lake Caller* and get some coverage, photos, too, of the chapter's effort to aid the police."

"That sounds like an attractive idea, Bruno. Well done! You're the likely candidate to head and organize the search.

He stopped as I held up my hand.

"What's wrong?"

"I was going to suggest it would be a super project for the Canyon Lake Boy Scout troop. The publicity could also boost the troop's membership."

Glasser shook my hand, the one I'd just used to stop him.

"Bingo! Both our chapter and the scouts benefit! That's a great idea!

"You want to organize the search effort, Bruno?"

I squirmed. "I'd rather the Scoutmaster and his scouts get the credit. Besides, I have another idea to run by you, if you can spare me another moment."

"Please, Bruno, go ahead. You're knocking the ball out of the old idea park. Let's hear it."

"This one involves the two of us, Herb. If you don't like it, just say so and it's forgotten. Okay?"

Glasser looked at me expectantly, so I plowed ahead. "I think you and I should search another area for Hugh Grimes, your predecessor as chapter president.

"Where is he?" I continued, looking Herb in the face. "It's been at least a week since he went missing. The public knows he's gone and the police have no clue. His wife is understandably at wit's end over his disappearance. She's numb from badgering the police and recently hired a private investigator to find him.

"I think finding Hugh Grimes is a bigger priority and help to the police than the Boy Scouts searching the beach."

"Okay, okay," Glasser checked his watch as if he had an appointment elsewhere. "What is your idea?"

"You either have seen or have an idea where is Hugh's favorite fishing spot. Why don't you and I jump in a vehicle and go look for it? You remember how to get there?"

"Well, yeah, I guess so. Say we luckily find his favorite fishing spot. What then? We bring him back to town, home and wife?

"I know Hugh pretty well. I can't imagine he would welcome us with open arms if we suddenly showed up there, presuming we can find 'there."

"You're suggesting he wouldn't come?" I asked.

"Never can tell. Maybe he's hiding from his wife and doesn't want to be found. Maybe he's got a playmate?" Herb raised his eyebrows suggestively.

"Then we'll just see if Hugh and his little red car are there and speed back to town and broadcast his whereabouts, like Paul Revere."

"Hugh may be armed, you know," Herb added another caution.

"You, his good friend and fellow chapter member, think he's dangerous?"

"I think we'd better be wary, is all I'm saying. Maybe I'm gun shy…"

Herb paused, thinking, for a full minute. "Hell! Let's do it!

"If we go now, it ought to be dark by the time we find him. If we can!"

TWENTY FOUR

ON THE NORTH SHORE OF CANYON LAKE

WEDNESDAY P.M

Herb was right about the fading light. It was dark when we reached a narrow, caliche road skirting the north side of the lake. Herb sat in the SUV passenger seat, telling me go slower or faster, as he tried to remember the location of Hugh's favorite fishing hole.

"That looks familiar," he pointed to a side road, ending in a cattle guard, a chained gate and barbed wire fence.

"Stop here," he whispered. "Better turn off the lights. If I'm right, it could be just over that rise," he gestured to the left.

"Go easy opening the doors." That got my attention since I'd been noticing the loud creaking every time I opened one.

We finally got over the barbed wire by holding up the top wire, while the other person climbed through it and number two. The cool breeze stopped and I was sweating in my denim shirt, probably as profusely as Herb.

"No more talking," he whispered. "Hugh may have trip wires out here. He used to have dogs, too. If we're lucky, the dogs are gone or maybe getting fed."

For the last fifty yards up the rise, we were crawling on hands and knees in the sage and sand fleas. It seemed like Viet Nam instead of Texas.

Another fifteen yards and we were at the crest of the rise. A wooden building, almost hidden, stood about fifty yards down the slope. No lights, at least on this side of the building. Behind the building there seemed to be a small shed.

Herb pointed at the dark structures. I couldn't see his face in the dark but his voice gave him away. He was completely surprised that he'd found the place so easily.

"Damn. I didn't know he had sheds out here! Looks like two of them." he whispered. We both were breathing hard.

"What now?" I whispered. "Do we knock on the front door, if there is one, or do we risk being shot?"

Herb lifted his hands like a winning prize fighter and motioned to the smaller shed. Silently, we crawled into it.

The shed was just three walls covered by a dark canvas top. Inside was a black shape covered by more canvas.

I lifted a corner of the canvas and there was Hugh's famous little red sports car.

We grinned like polecats until we heard a door at the front of the larger shed being opened.

Silently, we dropped to the ground and crawled back over the rise. Within long minutes, we reached the SUV. We pushed it, without engine or headlights, back the way we had come.

Once we were on the paved road and driving back to town, visible on the other side of the lake, Herb exclaimed, "We made it!

"I was a mite scared there for a minute," he admitted. "You, too?"

I relaxed with a fond memory. "I feel just like I've safely returned from a long range combat patrol to Long Hai, Viet Nam."

Herb was first to yell, once we were on the paved road, driving to the town. "Whooee! We found his place and his car! We made it!

"Lucky you found his place and got us in and out, Herb. Unnoticed, you think?"

Laughing with glee, Herb whooped again. "I think so. Thank God we weren't seen or heard! Stop at the first joint you can find, and I'm buying us a drink or two!"

"Third and fourth are on me!" I responded.

TWENTY FIVE

CANYON LAKE

THURSDAY

Our breakfast coffee that morning at a local cafe was interrupted by a newsboy loudly hawking the morning edition of the newspaper. It boasted another red head line:

'LADY IN RED"FOUND AT LAKE
FINALLY IDENTIFIED
WEDNESDAY AS MS. BERNICE
BANKS OF DALLAS. POLICE
INVESTIGATING DEATH AS
POSSIBLE HOMICIDE

I bought us a cheerful breakfast early that morning. After our third cup of coffee, we turned serious.

"What now?" Herb asked.

I reminded him. "We said we'd tell the police and Mrs. Grimes where Hugh is hiding Can you draw a sketch map of how to get to that shelter or whatever it's called? Since his car was in the smaller shed, he must have been in the larger one. Give one of your sketches to Chief Rogers, courtesy of your retired officers chapter, remind him. I'll give the other to Lois, his wife. That's what my partner, Abbie, and I promised her. Then maybe she and I can go home and resume our lives."

"Well," Herb hesitated. "What if the wife asks you about his health?

"I'll say we saw his red car. But not Hugh, whom we thought was inside the larger shed, presumably well."

"Huh," Herb thought again. "What if she asks you about …you know…was a female there, too?"

"Simple. I didn't see any female, did you?"

I dropped Herb at home and drove to 101 Lake View. On the way, I wondered if I was in a hurry to see Abbie or to tell Lois we knew where her husband was hiding.

My question was quickly answered as Abbie ran to the SUV and practically dragged me out.

"I missed you, cowboy!"

I hugged her hard and kissed her soundly. "I'm mighty tickled to see you, Boss!"

"Forget that 'Boss' stuff," she insisted. "Let's find someplace where we can talk about us."

Arms around each other, we made it as far as the cactus garden, a short distance from Lois's big house. Abbie pulled me down on a bench, suddenly serious.

"I overheard something mighty strange between Lois and that San Antonio detective she hired."

"I've got news, too," I blurted. "Herb and I found his secret shack on the north side of the lake and…"

Abbie held up her hand. "Me first," she insisted. "I think Hugh and his shack are no longer important to Lois."

"Why?"

"I was in the kitchen and overheard them on the telephone."

I was confused. "Who? Lois and Hugh?"

"Lois and that guy in San Antonio!" Impatient, she punched me.

"Listen to me carefully," she followed with another punch.

"She said if Hugh is hiding out somewhere with another woman, she didn't give a damn if he came home or not!"

"She was mad as hell!"

"The man asked, 'Do you mean I'm free to handle him as I see fit?"

That got my attention. Catching my breath, I asked, "What was her answer?"

"She told him, do as you please, but I want no fallout on me, the estate or the insurance policies. Understood?"

"Perfectly," he said. "I'll take personal care of this immediately!"

"How do you know where he is at this moment?"

"That's the sort of thing I do so well, Lois. Now, repeat the following after me: 'I have no idea of the location of Hugh's favorite fishing spot. He never told me. I didn't even know he liked to fish or that he had such a spot!"

Dutifully, she repeated his words.

"Another thing, Lois. This is unpleasant but vitally important. You and I must have absolutely no contact for at least six months, starting now!"

She gasped, "You mean it? Six months?"

"I don't like it, either, but it's necessary for appearances, my lovely grieving widow lady."

"I got it. You're a smart man, Don. I like that."

He continued. "Also for appearances, you will receive an invoice from my company to cover our services for Hugh's case. Pay it and keep your cashed check as a permanent record."

"My, you're thorough," she said. "I admire that, too.

"Six months from now is July," she counted. "Like to travel with a grieving widow lady?"

"You bet! What a couple we'll make!"

"Then I'll book us on a long Caribbean cruise. Find your passport! 'Bye for six months, lover!"

Abbie shivered. "I heard their entire conversation and I'm scared to death!"

I squeezed her hand. "Well done, sweetie. Sounds like our news about the location of his shack and red car no longer interest your old room mate. We might as well pack up and go home after telling the police what you heard."

"Not so fast!" Abbie frowned. "What about our reason for coming here? Remember, my design project to improve both her residence and my balance sheet?"

Somewhere else in Lois's residence, another telephone was quietly being hung up.

Both boots on his office desk, I caught my former hooch-mate, now Police Chief Chester Rogers by surprise.

"Who let you in?" he bellowed.

He stood and waved the sketch map to Hugh Grimes' fishing shack in my face, demanding "What am I supposed to do with this?"

Without being invited, I sat down in the fancy visitor chair in front of his desk and relaxed. This made Chester even madder.

Without hesitating, I asked the question.

"Chester, haven't you solved the case of the missing businessman yet? He's been missing for almost a week. The retired officer chapter has given you a free gift. Follow that sketch map and you'll find your missing businessman and close the case. Congratulations!

"By the way, you owe a mighty big thank you to Herb Glasser and his chapter. That sketch map solves your case!"

Chester resumed his chair and squinted at me.

"This sketch proves he isn't missing, doesn't it? Why do I want him? Has he committed some crime by going fishing without telling his wife?"

"I think Lois, his wife, would appreciate your report on finding her husband," I retorted. "She's a registered voter, able to influence hundreds of other voters in this county. Or are you considering early retirement, Chester?

"If you don't do your duty, I'm sure Rose, your favorite reporter, will find Hugh and write another front page story, even mentioning your inaction, Police Chief.

"Remember her 'Lady in Red' headline last week?"

Grinning at me, Rogers put his boots back on the desk.

"Listen to me, Bruno! The husband will go home when he gets hungry enough and dirty enough. That doesn't sound like a story meriting a big New York-style, red headline, does it?

"Now, get the hell outa' my office!"

TWENTY SIX

NORTH SIDE OF THE LAKE

THURSDAY

It was a dry summer in the Texas Hill country, heavily forested with cedar and oak. Due to the season, the fire tower at Canyon Lake had to be manned 24 hours a day by volunteers. Otis Weiner, the volunteer on night duty, saw the flames first, triangulated their location on the north rim of the lake and rang the fire alarm. It was heard as far away as San Marcos in the next county.

After giving the coordinates to the Fire Chief, Otis watched the night shift pour out of their barracks, suited up and ready to fight a fire.

"Burning real good," the Fire Chief said, using binoculars, "but it shouldn't be hard to get our water tenders close enough to put it out."

He jumped into his jeep and followed the now-manned fire truck to the coordinates pinpointed on the far side of the lake. The coordinates weren't necessary since the flames were plainly evident for miles around. The loud wail of the truck's siren awakened even the deepest sleepers in town. Soon other sirens could be heard throughout the three county area. Four volunteer fire departments had been alerted and were on the way to the rapidly spreading, highly visible, dangerous fire.

Among the emergency vehicles competing for space on the narrow road leading to the fire, was the jeep of the Police Chief Rogers of Canyon Lake.

"This is just like the damned Army," he groused to driver, John Sullivan. "On call 24-7! I should have taken the postal exam and had a quiet, pleasant mail route somewhere other than here."

He radioed the control room back at the police station. "Call county for the names of property owners on that stretch of the north lakeside. The fire department ambulance is probably on its way out there already, but check to make sure.

"If the hospital emergency room hasn't been alerted about possible casualties, tell them. Also call our medical examiner that we may have casualties out here. We haven't reached the burning area yet, so we don't know if there may be casualties.

"Watch that deep ditch, John!" he cautioned the driver. "Get us into that and we might not get out until noon."

Once arrived, Rogers assigned a traffic control team to man the entrance to the already congested area. The road and trails were full of firemen, dragging hoses and heavier equipment toward the fire.

"What can you tell me, Fire Chief?" Police Chief Rogers asked as he dismounted the jeep.

They walked toward the flames and stopped as the fire chief began pointing. "We have a small building and shed still blazing and almost destroyed. One tanker crew is working on the east side of both structures and one water tender crew is deployed on the opposite side.

"I plan to smother the burning buildings and concentrate all remaining teams on hosing down the woods around us. We've got to contain further burn. This whole area could go up in flames if we aren't successful."

Rogers grimaced and asked, "Could there be anyone trapped inside those buildings?"

"Don't know," the Fire Chief lifted his hands. "I hope not. Those building are too hot to send anybody, even fully-suited fire fighters, inside to look. I can't afford senseless losses."

The two were joined by Doctor Mills, the medical examiner, who nodded sadly. "I'll stand by and explore with you, Chief, once the buildings are cooler. From the noise and racket, I'd say more fire trucks are on the way."

The traffic control team called Chief Rogers. "We've got a big TV van complete with a female reporter out here wanting entry. What do I tell her, Chief?"

"Keep her out! This is an emergency situation until these fires are contained. Tell her to go home. We'll have a press conference, maybe, at 2:00 p.m. at the courthouse."

"Roger that, Chief, but she won't like it."

Minutes later, although it seemed like hours, Rogers had the information on who owned the burning structures.

"A Hugh Grimes of Canyon Lake pays the property taxes on that place, Chief, so he must be the owner."

"Hugh Grimes! He's our other active case. He's been missing since last Tuesday. Call his wife and see if he's come home."

"If he's not there?"

Rogers wiped his brow with a sleeve. "Just tell her we're still looking for her husband. Don't tell her about this fire. Might spook her and she'd come running out here."

The traffic control team called Rogers again. "Rose, that reporter, wants to speak to you, Chief."

"Tell her again," Rogers growled. "The press conference is planned for two p.m. at the court house. I can't talk to her now!"

"She wants to know if she can send in a photographer?"

"Hell no!" Rogers slammed down the telephone.

Doctor Mills and the Fire Chief were arguing next to a water trailer being towed into position beside Mills' gray mortuary van.

"Can you risk a team inside the big building yet?"

"Too hot, Doc. Are you that anxious for work? We've already been in that small shed next to the larger structure and it was extremely hot."

"What did you find?"

"Only casualty there was a blackened little sports car with Texas tags."

"Do we know the name of the registered owner?"

"Sure. The police control center tells us the owner of the car is the same Hugh Grimes, who owns this property."

"Then he must be inside?"

"Could be. We'll know when that building cools. Patience! You soon may have a customer, Doc!"

In a town café, Abbie and I looked at each other over a second cup of coffee. "The whole town can see that fire on the other side of the lake." Abbie said. "Lois must be aware of it, too.

"What can we tell her? She may not even know Hugh has a secret hide-away over there. Maybe her husband's been hiding out there since Tuesday!"

Abbie squeezed my hand. "You actually saw his place over there, right? Why didn't you go inside?"

"Yeah, Herb and I found it. Herb didn't want to knock on the door, thinking we might be unwelcome and get shot. We never saw Hugh, but his little red car was nearby, all covered up by canvas.

I returned to our table after paying the check. "All I can think to do is, return to her house and stay with Lois until we know if Hugh was injured."

Abbie grabbed her shoulder bag. "That's weak, Bruno, but I don't have a better idea. Let's go."

As usual, Grace met us at the front door as we ascended the steps. "Do you know what's happening in town?"

"Big fire on the other side of the lake, Grace. How's Lois?"

Grace shook her head. "She's acting strange, very quiet and thoughtful, like the time that man called her from San Antonio.

"She's already had a call from the police. I heard them ask her if Hugh had returned home. Can you imagine such a question? Is there some connection between Hugh and that fire?

"Go upstairs and give her more medicine. Maybe that will make her happier. You always are able to improve her mood."

Upstairs, Lois relaxed on the big leather couch, smoking a cigarette and finishing one of her famous margaritas. Accenting the Mexican mood, the CD was loudly playing mariachi music. As they knocked, she yelled, "C'mon in!"

"Sit, sit," she pointed to the big couch. "Let's liven up this dull place!"

She reached for the phone. "Grace! More margaritas please… and snacks, too."

We looked at each other in surprise. What happened to the calm, thoughtful Lois, just described by Grace downstairs?

Uncertain how to begin, Abbie sat down next to Lois and said, "Grace told us the police called and asked if Hugh had come home."

Lois tittered. "Dumb question. Typical of our police. They also said something about a fire at the lake. What's up? Is here some connection between Hugh and a fire?"

I looked at Abbie. She nodded at me to answer.

"Lois, the police say a shed on the north side of the lake is burning and that shed belongs to Hugh."

"Ridiculous! As far as I know Hugh's never been on that side of the lake. A shed? He would never keep such a secret from me! I know him too well!"

"We hope Hugh is okay wherever he is, Lois," Abbie came to my rescue. "But there's a chance that Hugh may involved in that fire. If the burning shed is his, he may have been injured!"

Grace entered with a loaded silver tray.

Frowning at Abbie's words, Lois pointed to the table. "Put it over there, Grace, and pour us all a drink. You, too! Did you hear what Abbie just said?"

"Yes, M'am, I did. I hope your husband is alright, just missing."

"Grace, did Hugh ever mention a shed or anything he had on the north side of the lake?"

Before answering, Grace sat in a nearby chair and looked at Abbie, then me.

"No, M'am, I don't think so. Perhaps I better go fetch your medicine now?"

Lois shook her head. "No, no. Relax. Finish your drink. After we finish this pitcher of margaritas, I'm going to mix another of my specials. And the four of us are going to drink it all!"

TWENTY SEVEN

NORTH SIDE OF THE LAKE

THURSDAY

Chief Rogers sat in the van with Doctor Mills. The medical examiner kept looking at his watch. "Do you think the buildings have cooled enough yet?

"Don't worry, Doc. The Fire Chief will tell us as soon as the building's safe enough to enter and investigate. There also may be structural damage to the building making it hazardous longer than we want to wait."

Rogers glanced at his sweating companion. "Doc, why don't we get out there near the water, where it's a bit cooler? I see a small boat in the water over there. Let's go sit in it. We'll be much cooler than here."

Doctor Mills shrugged. “Sure, Chief. That beats sitting in this hot van, wondering who or what’s left inside that shed.”

Together they walked to the small boat.

“If this fire turns into a homicide, Chief, should we be getting in this boat? It might contain evidence of some kind.”

“Maybe, Doc. All I can see in it is some rope attached to a gunnel.”

“A rope?” Mills’ voice bristled with interest and he hurried over.

“Yeah!” he cried, holding up a wet length of rope. “A rope! Maybe the very one I’ve been looking for!”

The fire team was the first to enter the burned shed to determine the cause of the fire. An hour later, they exited, holding up a burned, otherwise new appearing electrical switch.

“Here’s the culprit!” the Fire Chief exclaimed, detailing a fire guard to remain until evening, to assure no flare-ups.

“All yours, Chief Rogers!” The crime scene team borrowed from Comal County entered the shed as the fire team left, closely followed by Doctor Mills and his two assistants in black coveralls.

Initially, there was little to see in the burned–out shed but black smoke. In a far corner had been an old-fashioned television, now a smoking hulk of plastic. A butane stove remained upright in the mist of debris from a collapsed kitchen counter.

"Look at this." Doctor Mills touched Rogers' sleeve. He stood beside the remains of a old-fashioned iron bed, its ivory finish burned black.

On the burned bed was a blackened human body, sprawled amid burned sheets and smoking blankets.

Chief Rogers quickly backed away, holding a handkerchief over his nose. "Is…was… that our missing Hugh Grimes, Doc?"

Doctor Mills shook his head, closely peering at the burned body with a penlight.

"Can't tell until I get the body into our lab for a real exam. Fingerprints may not help since the hands are as badly burned as the face and torso. Maybe we can find his dental records."

Rogers was exploring the floor with the toe of his boot. "Look what I found over here."

With a pencil from his pocket, he picked up an empty bottle from the floor. Trying to read the burned label, he squinted. "Grey Goose. Isn't that vodka?"

Unable to separate the body from the burned bed, Mills closely watched as his gloved assistants carefully carried both to the grey van.

Four hours later, the Police Chief, Fire Chief and Doctor Mills sat around a long table in the Comal County courthouse. Minutes later they were joined by the District Attorney, and representatives of the Texas Rangers and FBI. After hurried introductions and hand shakes, Chief Rogers stood and glanced at the others.

"I come from a 'take charge' background, so I'll begin, unless somebody has a better idea.

"We are here to initially hear the cause of this fire from our Fire Chief," he nodded at his seat mate, "and then the cause of death." He glanced at Doctor Mills.

"Finally we must determine if this casualty, just identified as Mr. Hugh Grimes of Canyon Lake, was the result of an accident or a criminal act.

"Everyone in agreement so far?" Rogers asked the serious faces around the table.

The Fire Chief arose and Rogers sat down.

"My initial opinion was that this fire was the result of a faulty electrical switch. This one." He held up the questionable switch.

"Later, we checked an old electrical plan for the shed that we luckily found. Tracing the schematic, we discovered an external, severed hot wire. How was it severed? Well, it looked like it had been recently cut.

"That hot wire created a spark, igniting a stack of old newspapers. We found no traces of accelerant but the newspapers were enough to smolder and burn brightly. The dry condition of the shed did the rest."

A Texas Ranger seated at the table raised his hand. "Did you just describe an accidental fire or did someone start it?"

The Fire Chief nodded and sat down. "I think it was deliberate. Unfortunately, this fire is typical of many in older buildings in the country, especially abandoned ones."

Chief Rogers also sat down as opinions were bandied about the table. No general agreement was reached. After several more minutes of discussion and debate, the Fire Chief held up his hand and read from his notes.

"I'm concluding my report with the following. 'Origin of the fire remains suspicious, the result of deliberate action by party or parties unknown.' Let's see the hands of anyone who objects to that."

Despite several frowns, no hands were raised. Police Chief Rogers stood again. "If new evidence is found by the Fire Chief, we can revisit his conclusion. Now, Doctor Mills, will you tell us your decision about the cause of death?"

Following the others, Mills arose. "Cause of death was severe burns over seventy percent of the body of the deceased male. Obviously, there were severe burns and contusions all over the body. Among them was an odd indentation on the bottom of the right foot, possibly a syringe mark. The casualty was in bed, supine, apparently sleeping, when the shed caught fire."

The Ranger raised a hand. "Was he awake? If so, why didn't he attempt to get out?"

"May I, Doctor?" Chief Rogers stood.

"Sure, Chief. Go ahead. Tell them."

"Am empty vodka bottle was found beside the bed. The victim may have been inebriated and unable to get out of bed, much less out of the building. Another bottle, a full one, same brand, was found in his burned car."

The same Texas Ranger asked, "Conclusion, Doctor?"

"Suspicious death due to conflagration," Mills looked at his notes. "Questions?"

"What could have caused that indentation on the foot other than a syringe, Doctor?"

Mills nodded. "I've been puzzling with that question since I found it. I have no answer, thus my use of the word 'Suspicious."

There were puzzled looks but no further questions, so Mills sat down.

"Your turn, Chief Rogers," he said.

Rogers placed both hands on the table and stared at the others. "The fire may not have been started accidentally. The severed wire speaks to that.

"If the deceased was drunk, his death could have been accidental, were it not for the mark on the bottom of one foot. The mark or indentation may have been caused by a needle.

"My conclusion is homicide."

For the first time, the District Attorney stood, glaring at the others. "Considering what we've heard here from these gentlemen, no court would hear such a flimsy case! It would never come to trial! Laughable! There's not even an accused!"

Back in Chief Roger's office, he, the Fire Chief and Doctor Mills sat around the department's conference table, drinking coffee.

"Ever want a job, Betty, come to the Fire Department. Your java's better than ours."

Rogers jumped out of his chair. "Betty, if you decide to leave me, please give me an hour's notice so I can arrange a big, stay-with-me bonus!"

TWENTY EIGHT

CANYON LAKE

THURSDAY

Once the coffee pot was empty, Rogers introduced investigator Larry Francis to the Fire Chief. “Larry’s been working the case of the ‘Lady in Red,’ that you’ve read about. I’ve asked him to go over his findings about her death. You will remember her drowned body was found washed up on a beach not far from where we sit.”

“Thank you, Chief,” Larry began. ‘The Lady in Red’ was finally identified as Ms. Bernice Stone of Dallas, age 30, occupation--according to Dallas Police, who shared her file with us--cocktail hostess. The bright red panties and bra she was wearing when found on the beach were instrumental in her identification.

"She arrived in Canyon Lake on the Dallas bus late Monday night. The bus company has been unable to provide us a passenger list. Luckily, Ms. Stone's bright red fingernails attracted the bus ticket seller's attention. They had a conversation about her fingernail color. Ms. Stone asked directions to Fifth Street and left the station.

"Mr. Hugh Grimes' red sports car was seen at the Texaco gas station that night and the attendant remembered Grimes' mentioning Fifth Street as he left.

"Supposition One: Grimes and Ms. Stone had arranged to meet at Fifth Street that night once her bus arrived.

"Back to the Texaco station attendant. He heard the noise of Grime's red sport car, shifting gears and leaving town at a high speed in the direction of the lake.

"We now know that Grimes' had a fishing shed on the opposite side of the lake which no one, not even his wife, knew about. That's the larger building or shed just destroyed by fire.

"Supposition Two: Grimes and Stone spent the night in his fishing shed on the north side of the lake. His wife was unaware of her husband's absence that night, or any other night. She usually goes to bed at nine, she says. Often her husband is out all night, but back in bed by morning when she awakes.

"Supposition Three: Grimes and Stone began arguing about something in the shed. The argument turned violent, ending in a deadly fight. Stone was killed, perhaps accidentally, perhaps not.

"Grimes probably panicked and decided the best way to get rid of her body. He carried her to his fishing boat docked nearby. Next, he paddled her across the lake, and dumped the body on the beach near here, where she was found the next morning.

"Yes, Doctor?"

"I may be able to add to your analysis, Larry. I found several lesions on the ankles of Ms. Stone the next day. Her ankles appeared to have been tied together by a rope. I submit that Grimes towed her body, behind his boat, to the opposite shore of the lake where she was found."

"Thank you, Doctor. That could explain how she could have been quietly transported, during darkness, remember, from the opposite side of the lake where she was killed by Grimes.

"Whew! No wonder there were no clues on the beach where her body was found! Any clues were on the opposite side of the lake at his fishing shed or in his boat!"

"Lots of suppositions there, Larry," Rogers scratched his forehead. "But you may have solved the murder of 'The Lady in Red."

'Now, what shall we do about it?" Rogers frowned.

Doctor Mills pyramided his fingers. "Later, the murderer was himself murdered. That means we have yet another murder to solve."

"Yeah," Francis rolled his eyes. "So, who killed the murderer?"

TWENTY NINE

CANYON LAKE

THURSDAY P.M.

Abbie and I sat in the rose garden before joining Lois for dinner. Grace approached with a telephone.

"For you," she handed it to me. "It's Chief Rogers."

"Bruno here," I answered. "Haven't heard from you lately, buddy. Did we declare an armistice?"

"Cut the funny stuff, Bruno. I need your help right away."

"Once a hooch-mate, always a hooch-mate. What may I do for you?"

"I'm already on the way to the Grimes' place, to deliver bad news to Mrs. Grimes."

I motioned at Abbie to listen. "You found him?"

"Yes."

"Alive …"

"No, dead."

I couldn't disguise my surprise. "Dead?"

"Yeah. Now listen. I need you and Abbie to be with her when I arrive there to tell her. I'm not good at dead notifications. Never was, especially in Viet Nam.

"She's likely to go haywire, poor thing. Being friends, you and Abbie may be able to comfort her in some way.

"I'm almost at her front door. Help me, please!"

Abbie shut her eyes and squeezed my arm. "We'll do what we can. She said if he was off with another woman, she didn't want him to come home...but dead? I don't know how she'll react."

"Let's go to the dining table because Grace just opened the front door for Rogers.

Abbie rushed to Lois' side. "Dear, Chief Rogers is here with news about Hugh."

Lois sat straighter in her chair and glared at approaching Rogers. "So you've finally come to tell me where my husband is, have you? How long has it been, almost two weeks?"

"Yes, M'am. I regret that my news is not good." Rogers awkwardly stood before her, hat in hand.

Lois shut her eyes and gripped Abbie's hand. "Well, spit it out! Where is he?"

"I'm very sorry to report that your husband died in a fire on the north side of the lake. We just found him. M'am, I'm extremely..."

Lois' scream cut him short. "Oh, God! No, no, no! Not my Hugh! You must be mistaken! It must be someone else! How can you be certain?"

She lapsed into choking and crying, Abbie continued to hug her tightly. Once the crying and wailing abated, Grace helped Lois out of the chair and announced, "I'm taking her upstairs, giving her some medicine and calling the doctor."

Chief Rogers, my Viet Nam buddy, looked like he needed medication, too. I poured him a cup of coffee.

"No, thanks, Bruno. Thanks to you and Abbie for being here to help. I've got to get back to town right away to organize the press meeting about this mess. See you later."

Abbie nodded as I refilled her cup and sat down beside her. She looked at me thoughtfully and asked, "Did you see Grace's face as she took Lois upstairs?"

"Sure. What did Grace do that caught your attention at such a time?"

"She winked at me!"

As expected, the next edition of *THE CANYON LAKE CALLER* began with another larger-than-life red headline:

MISSING MAN FOUND DEAD
IN BURNING HIDEAWAY

The accompanying article reviewed Thursday's press briefing at the courthouse. The conclusions of the Fire Chief, Medical Examiner and Police Chief were mentioned briefly.

In contrast, the District Attorney's remarks were quoted verbatim, leaving the question of 'was it homicide or accident?' Also on the front page were photos of Hugh Grimes and the burned-out shed in which he was found.

THIRTY

CANYON LAKE

A WEEK LATER

The week was hectic yet pleasurable. For a change, Abbie and I spent time together, free from worries about finding Hugh Grimes. Lois spent most of her time in her room, faithfully attended by Grace. Occasionally, we had meals together, usually breakfast.

Lois was happy to leave the coordination and arranging of Hugh's funeral to us. Without a clear mandate from grieving Lois, Abbie's interior design and decoration plans remained on hold.

One of our first chores was to coordinate with church, funeral home, cemetery and newspaper to announce the date, place and time of the service for Hugh.

Lois was in her room most days, presumably grieving. We seldom saw her during that week.

Finally, our coordination was complete and the service schedule printed in *The Canyon Lake Caller.*

Both Abbie and I had to quickly retreat to our respective homes to pick up appropriate clothing for a funeral, and check on our neglected businesses. We rushed back to Canyon Lake in time for the funeral service we planned.

That night Abbie and I were having one of Lois' famous margaritas with our hostess. Lois said, "I appreciate what you two are doing for me." She raised her glass to us.

"You two are a marvel. I could have never made it through this nightmare without your love and support."

The day before the service, Abbie, Grace and I selected flowers to be delivered to the church. Grace insisted on paying for the attractive display she selected.

We also went to the cemetery to see the impressive tombstone erected years before for both Hugh and Lois.

Grace began to cry. "I owe Mr. Grimes much more than an attractive floral tribute," she sobbed.

"What's wrong, Grace!"

She blanched. "I don't feel free to tell you at the moment. It's my problem and I must solve it by myself."

"If we can help, we're here," I patted her arm.

After a few moments, Grace shut her eyes. "Remember when Lois said if there was another woman with Hugh, she didn't care if he came home?"

"I remember," Abbie said. "But I don't think she meant it. She was just angry."

Grace grabbed another tissue. "Oh, yes. She meant it! I know there have been other things--unbelievable things--she said that really shocked me. After twelve years working for the Grimes, not much shocks me anymore."

Abbie and I sat stone-faced, uncertain we wanted to hear about the unbelievables.

Grace continued, "I need to rationally think about Lois' words and decide what's best for me to do. If anything."

At that, she lowered her head and wept again.

The day of Hugh's funeral was ominous with dark clouds and thunder on the horizon. The parking lot at St. Barnabas' Church was full before ten o'clock, for a service expected to begin at noon. The four of us, Lois, Abbie, Grace and I, arrived early in Lois's new Lexus.

The entire town turned out, either to honor the departed or see his grieving widow. Hugh's business associates, church board members, Kiwanis, Rotary, City Council and golf foursome, plus many others, all attended.

Lois' friends, filling the front aisles, included the flower and garden clubs, Church Circle, the local DAR, and the independent school board. Smiling slightly, she acknowledged them, taking her seat in the front with us. She was quiet and thoughtful during the service. The later interment would be private, family-only.

Abbie sat next to Lois during the long service, holding her hand, and offering occasional tissues. At the conclusion, we accompanied Lois out the front door where the pastor held Lois' hand and whispered encouragement.

Next we entered the nearby church hall, where refreshments were offered, along with more hand shaking and mumbled condolences. Lois soon tired of this and we took her and Grace home in the Lexus.

THIRTY ONE

CANYON LAKE

THE FOLLOWING THURSDAY

Lois, Abbie and I enjoyed a late breakfast by the pool. Idle talk repeated bits of politics, weather, and the economy gleaned from the morning TV. We studiously avoided mention of Hugh.

"It was just like our arrival here that first day," Abbie said later, when we were alone upstairs in her room. "There was no mention of Hugh that day, either. We sat there like first termers at summer camp."

"You don't remember?" I chided. "That first day you had plenty on your mind, like an eleven o'clock briefing the next morning on your design proposal for her big house.

"When or if, are you reviving that subject, or are we just going to say thanks and adios, Canyon Lake?"

She stuck out her tongue. "I told you before, remember? We need to pursue our original purpose in coming here. Continuing our project at her residence might help her adjust to suddenly being a widow."

"And provide you a career enhancer?" I asked shyly.

She frowned. "Yeah, that, too, but only if Lois wants us around. We may be ingrained in her memory of bad times here. If so, we must go home."

I sat up straighter. "You said we must leave. Does that mean you and I part and go our separate ways like before?"

Abbie leaned forward on the bed where we sat and kissed me. "Does that answer that silly question, cowboy?"

It was an unexpected, 'bingo' kiss so I kissed her right back, even more passionately. "At last we're back to where we were years ago. I didn't want to part then, nor now..."

My sentence stopped since she rolled over on me and kissed me like never before.

When we came up for air, we heard someone pounding on the door.

Still breathless, we untangled and I answered the door.

It was Grace.

"Are you deaf?" she demanded. "I've been out here knocking for...." she checked her watch, "three whole minutes."

The lipstick smudges on me answered her question.

"Oh, sorry! I'll come back later...or maybe in the morning?"

Abbie, always cool and collected, gestured.

"Come on in, Grace. We were just playing a little gin rummy," Abbie giggled.

"I can see that," Grace nodded, poker-faced "Are you sure this is a good time 'cause I need to talk seriously to you both."

I pulled up a chair and seated her. "Coffee, Grace? I'll make some in the microwave here."

"No, no." Grace took a deep breath. "This is about the other day when I said there is something really bothering me. Remember?"

"Sure, we remember," Abbie and I replied in unison. "Tell us what's wrong."

She seemed to relax slightly. "Okay. Yes, to the coffee offer," she wiped her eyes. "Maybe coffee will help me say the right words and make some sense."

After I heated and served us three cups of instant coffee, we sat and looked at each other. No smiles.

"First," she stared at us. "I need your promises that what I tell you will not…will not…be shared with Lois. I owe her for my good life here.

"Do you both promise you will never tell Lois what I'm about to tell you?"

This suddenly was serious. Abbie and I looked at each other for a long minute. Then we both nodded. "We promise."

"I also owe Hugh, rest his soul, for years of helping not only me, but my mother as well. Hugh managed to get Mom into a senior nursing home where she receives great care. She's happy. I owe that to Hugh Grimes, a real gentleman.

"I confess that I'm a sneak, always wanting to know what's going on in this lovely residence. Maybe I think that's my duty as caretaker and companion?

"So, I often overhear people talking, or on the telephone, which I record in my notebook. A strange, wicked habit, I agree, a habit nonetheless.

"Now, the following are from the notes I took during the last conversation between Lois and that Mr. Drake of that detective agency in San Antonio.

"Are you ready to hear something both terrible and unbelievable?"

Abbie and I looked at each other, wide-eyed and held hands, as if we were about to watch a terror movie.

Grace drew a deep breath. "I remind you of your promises to never, never tell Lois!"

The tension Grace created made us both gulp, before agreeing again.

"Here goes," Grace began reading from her notebook.

Lois: If he's with another woman, I don't care if he ever comes home! He's all yours!

Drake: Do you mean I can handle him as I see fit?

Lois: Do as you please, but I want no fallout on me, the estate, or our insurance policies. Understood?

Drake: Perfectly. I'll take personal care of this matter.

Lois: Do you know where to find him?

Drake: This is the sort of thing I do well. Repeat after me, Lois, what I'm about to say. "I have no idea where Hugh's favorite fishing spot is. He never told me. I didn't even know he liked to fish or that he had a favorite spot."

Lois: She repeated his words.

Drake: For appearances, Lois, we must not see or contact each other for six months starting now. Also for appearances, you will receive a bill from my firm for services in this case. Pay the bill. Save your returned check as a permanent record.

Lois: In six months, would you like to travel the world with a grieving widow?

Drake: YES!

Lois: Great! I'll book us on a long Caribbean cruise to begin.

Grace sat down and covered her face. "I feel like a traitor to Lois but I don't see any other way out. My conscience will never let me rest if I do otherwise. Please, please try to understand and advise me what I should do.

"Now you can understand my distress. Hugh Grimes was no angel but he didn't deserve to be murdered by his wife and some stranger!

"Please tell me what I should do." she repeated, through tears.

THIRTY TWO

CANYON LAKE

THURSDAY P.M.

"We've got to get you out of here, Grace," I offered her another cup of instant coffee which she refused.

"Grace, are you willing to tell the Police Chief what you just told us?"

"Yes, I will, if you think that's the best thing to do," she nodded, drying tears again.

"Can you live for a while with a relative or close friend until this is settled?" Abbie asked. "Bruno and I will take you there right away, tonight."

"I could stay with my sister, Alice. She lives in town."

"In the past, who has replaced you here while you were vacationing or ill?"

Grace reached for another tissue. "Lois' sister, Eloise, has substituted for me in the past. She was always happy to do so for the salary. She manages a thrift shop downtown.

"If you can, Grace, why not call Eloise now and ask her to take your place here in the residence, starting tonight?"

"Okay, I'll call her now."

"Can you also call Alice and ask to stay with her? We'll take you there and bring Eloise back here."

Imagining our next step, Abbie said, "I'll go upstairs and tell Lois your mother is ill, needs you and asks you to come immediately. I'll also tell her we have arranged for Eloise to come here temporarily until you can return."

Grace murmured, "I pray I never have to return here!"

"Great work, Abbie!" I hugged her. "What are we missing?"

"Bruno, go with Grace to her room and help her pack for a long absence. Is that alright, Grace?"

Grace refused another tissue. "That's thoughtful. Yes, fine. I love you both for what you're doing. I'd never be able to do this by myself, especially go upstairs and face that woman."

At that, Abbie went upstairs to see Lois. Grace and I hurried to her room and we packed two suitcases with her belongings.

Twenty minutes later, Grace, Abbie and I were piling into the SUV and heading for town. Grace was welcomed by Alice, at her home in Canyon Lake. After introductions, we declined coffee and cake and were out the door to Eloise's apartment.

I hugged Grace. "We're coming back in the morning to take you to breakfast and talk about what we should do next. Okay?"

Abbie gave Grace a kiss and waved as we left for our next stop, Eloise's apartment three blocks away. Although it seemed much longer, we soon were back at the residence with an eager Eloise and her luggage.

"How did Lois react when you told her that Eloise was replacing Grace for a few days?"

"She exploded, but not because of that. Lois was going through Hugh's desk and found a mail order invoice that infuriated her. I've never seen her so mad. She went berserk!"

"What about?"

"Remember the red bra and panties on that girl's body at the beach?"

"Sure. The newspaper dubbed her 'The Lady in Red.'"

"Well, Hugh ordered **two** sets of those red bras and panties. One was for Lois, the other for the young girl whom he took to his secret north shore shed for a tryst, then killed her."

I frowned. "Lois caught Hugh red-handed, so to speak. No wonder she was pissed!"

Abbie glared at me as if I was the culprit "What woman wouldn't be? But that's not all. Lois said she was going to order more of the red panties and bra sets and dye her hair a flaming red!"

"I love the sheen and that shade of red against my body," she claimed. "I'm wearing red for the rest of my life, to hell with changing fashions!

"Red means mayhem, malice!" she shouted as I left. "And that's me!"

We both were strangely quiet on the way to Lois' home.

"Let's check into a quiet motel instead of dealing with Lois and her anger tonight?"

"Nice try, lover, but we need to be there to prevent her from burning the place down! She's so mad!"

By my watch, we had been gone only two and a half hours. We were back at Lois's residence, and in bed.

Solo, unfortunately.

THIRTY THREE

CANYON LAKE

FRIDAY

The courthouse parking lot, where the press conference was held, was already crowded with spectators by 1:00 p.m. Chairs were so scarce that many locals brought lawn chairs from their homes.

Chief Rogers stood at a microphone stand being lengthened for his height. Beside him were the Fire Chief, Medical Examiner, and the seldom-seen District Attorney.

Rogers read the statement with which the four had finally agreed.

"The Fire Department responded to a fire on the north side of the lake at approximately 2:00 a.m. this morning. Fire and pump trucks--including three from neighboring counties--were immediately dispatched to the distant location. Burning brightly at the arrival of our first responders were two small buildings.

"The fire teams immediately began extinguishing the blazes as well as cordoning off the adjoining wooded areas to prevent further fire and destruction.

"Once the fires were out and the destroyed buildings were judged safe enough to enter, a fire team inspected them. In the larger building, a body of a male was found. The male was later identified as Mr. Hugh Grimes, resident of Canyon Lake. The property destroyed also belonged to Mr. Grimes.

"The Medical Examiner's team removed the body for further examination at the Canyon Lake facility.

"We are indebted to the officials and fire departments of Kendall and Hays Counties who quickly came to our aid in this disaster."

Questioning hands were raised through out the crowd.

"What caused the fire?"

The Fire Chief stepped forward to answer. "We are still investigating the cause. Once determined, an announcement will be made."

"Was the second building destroyed as well?"

"Yes, it was."

"Were any people inside it?"

"No, only a vehicle belonging to Mr. Grimes, the victim."

"Has the next of kin been notified?"

Rogers answered. "Yes, next of kin, the victim's wife, was notified today."

"Was the death of Mr. Grimes an accident or a homicide" Rose, the local reporter for *The Canyon Lake Caller*, asked, aiming her recorder at the Police Chief.

The Chief began to answer but his microphone was grabbed by the previously silent District Attorney.

"There is no evidence that this tragedy was anything other than an accident. And you can print that!" He glared at the reporter.

The District Attorney continued to rant.

"The Fire Chief is still investigating to determine if the fire was accidental. The Medical Examiner is still examining the burn victim.

"Is there a witness to this tragedy? No! Was a criminal action committed? Not proven! If this was a criminal action, what was the motive? None determined! Is there a suspect? No!"

The District Attorney shook his head at further questioners and held up his hand. "This press conference is ended!"

His angry reaction irritated the crowd, many muttering, some slowly beginning to depart.

Rose walked over to Chief Rogers for his reaction.

"You just heard the chief law enforcement officer of this county. What can I say?"

THIRTY FOUR

CANYON LAKE

FRIDAY

Lois and Eloise were chatting and laughing over coffee and crumb cake. Abbie and I, holding hands, joined them on the terrace.

Lois noticed our hands and smiled, raising her eyebrows. "What are your plans?"

Abbie blinked at Lois' expectant look. "We just have some quick business in town this morning."

"Involving shopping for something special I bet?" Lois grinned.

"Great idea!" I exclaimed before Abbie could speak.

"No, nothing special," Abbie deferred. "We're just going to browse."

Once on our way to pick up Grace and have breakfast, plus a serious planning session, Abbie pinched me. "What did you mean back there about shopping?"

"Glad you asked," I pecked her on the cheek. "It's time we had a talk about our own future, instead planning everybody else's."

"Concentrate, cowboy, concentrate. Rope one calf at a time. Right now we have poor Grace to aid, if we can. What's your idea for her?"

"Nothing ingenious," I admitted. "We take her to my friend, the police chief, for a hearing. If he thinks there is enough evidence, we try it on that smug District Attorney.

"The D.A. said there is no motive for Hugh's death? What about that $500,000 policy on Hugh's life? He said there was no suspect?

"Hell, we have two! The widow and her co-conspirator in San Antonio!"

We picked up a tired-looking Grace at her sister's home. Grace had no favorite restaurant so we stopped for breakfast at a place called Country Kitchen.

We were quiet until the coffee was served. "Funny," Abbie looked at Grace. "Ever notice that conversations never start flowing until we've had a cup of coffee?"

"That's why politicians drink so much coffee," I offered, but no one laughed.

"Down to business," Abbie instructed. "Go, Bruno. Tell Grace your idea."

I pushed away my coffee. "I suggest I make an appointment with Chief Rogers and we go see him. You tell Rogers about that incriminating conversation you heard between Lois and that Drake guy. Bring your notebook, Grace, and tell the Chief just what you told us.

"If the Chief thinks there's enough evidence to convict, we repeat it to the District Attorney. Lois and Drake are arrested, awaiting trial. Grace's conscience is clear. Abbie and I continue our lives, except maybe for the design project briefing she didn't get to present."

Abbie puckered her lips, and smiled. "It's still a great project! Maybe the new owner will want to hear our presentation someday." She looked at me and grinned. "**Our** presentation."

"What do you think about Bruno's idea, Grace?"

"I lay awake all night but haven't come up with a better one. Is Chief Rogers a nice guy?"

"Not always 'nice,'" I admitted. "I've known him a long time. I'd say he's fair and honest."

Grace looked at Abbie. "What do you think?"

"Like you, I haven't a better solution, dear."

"Then, let's go see the Chief," Grace said, pushing aside her coffee.

Although we had no appointment, the Chief's door was open. We took that as a good omen and entered.

"Good morning, Chief," I startled him, reading the newspaper.

I expected his usual yell. "Who let this reject in here?"

Instead, he smiled as if he'd just been awarded a decoration. "Come in, come in."

"Chief, this is Ms. Grace Woodley, housekeeper and caretaker of Lois Grimes. Ms. Woodley overheard a plan between Mrs. Grimes and a Mr. Drake, of whom you've heard. Their plan, which Ms. Woodley recalls vividly and recorded in her notebook, was to murder Mr. Grimes. As you know, their plan succeeded. Mr. Grimes was murdered.

"Chief, you may need to make a formal record of Ms. Woodley's story,"

Grace spoke up. "Not a story, Chief. It's all true and please call me Grace."

"Thank you, Grace," he smiled broadly. "Just a minute," he held up a hand. "Let me get a stenographer in here to make a record of your testimony."

With that, Chester buzzed Betty for a stenographer and we all sat down. Grace seemed as calm as Abbie. I looked like I'd been steer-wrestling and the steer won.

Once joined by a steno and her machine, Grace began repeating, in a calm voice, what she'd told Abbie and me.

Occasionally, she glanced at her notebook. Her memory was astounding and her tone convincing.

The Chief asked few questions, allowing Grace's entire testimony to be captured by the steno.

Once Grace was finished, she breathed a sigh of relief. "Hope I never have to repeat that again," she whispered.

"You won't," Chester assured her, "But there will be lots of questions concerning the details of what you just said.

"Grace, our steno will leave and print out your testimony. It's important that you carefully review that testimony and correct any errors or mistakes. Why? Because you must formally attest to the absolute accuracy of your testimony, which will be used in a court of law."

Once the steno returned with the print-out of Grace's testimony, Chester handed it to her. "Take your time, Grace, all the time you need, to review every word printed here. Why? Because your words will be used in court, after we convince that District Attorney that we have a case.

Grace took her time in reviewing the print-out, making an occasional note or minor correction.

Chester asked, "Are you ready to swear before a notary public to the accuracy of this document?"

"I am, Chester," she smiled at him.

After two hours, Grace had completed her review and the notarization. "May we go now, Chester?" I asked.

"We're taking Grace to a nice dinner somewhere. She's been under lots of stress lately. We want to treat and relax her if we can."

Chester stood beside Grace and asked, "Is it okay if I come, too?"

She said, "Absolutely, Chester. Please come."

We said good bye to Betty, the secretary.

Chester turned. "Betty, would you please close up for me tonight?" He took Grace's arm and the four of us piled into the SUV.

Once at Lois' residence, Abbie and I relaxed with drinks by a small fire on the patio.

"I'm reminded that you promised to tell me about that nickname you earned in Viet Nam," she snuggled closer.

"Here we have drinks and a cozy fire, those were my only requisites" she said.

Abbie puckered her lips. "Go, Bruno! Tell me about how you earned that nickname, the 'Bitcher."

I took a long sip of the bourbon and water, thinking 'why did I ever open my mouth?'

She kicked me in the boot. "Start now, Bruno. Talk!"

"Okay, but this isn't much of a story. Viet Nam. Nobody wanted to be there. Everybody complained."

"Skip the long introduction, Bruno."

I took another sip from the glass. It was perspiring, just like me.

"It was the weather, among other things. During the monsoon season, everything, everybody was wet. If you made the mistake of washing your dirty socks, you might as well throw them away. They'd never be dry again. Dry toilet paper? A luxury!

"Coffee was always cold, the malarial pills hard to swallow, the mail, if there was some, always late. Warm showers? Nonexistent. Hamms beer? Never cold, if there had been a beer drop from the choppers.

"Please, please, tell me that's enough, Abbie."

'Okay, until the next time. But you're not off the hook yet, Bitcher!"

At the courthouse, the Office of the District Attorney was also closing for the day. A harried member of the DA's staff knocked on his door.

"Sorry, sir," he hesitated finishing his question since the DA was putting on his coat to depart.

"What is it, James?"

"Just received a request to add to your calendar tomorrow morning, sir."

"At what time?"

"The request is for ten o'clock, sir, and the Anders trial starts at eleven."

"Okay, put it on the calendar for thirty…no, twenty five minutes only. You look dubious. What's wrong?"

"Sir, the request is from Police Chief Rogers of Canyon Lake. He says he needs at least an hour and a half."

"That's absurd, just like a hick country cop. What's his subject? The weather?"

"He has new evidence on the Grimes case, sir."

"Not likely. He's just honking his horn. It's election time over at the lake. Give him twenty-five minutes. No more, understand?"

THIRTY FIVE

CANYON LAKE

SATURDAY

By ten o'clock, we sat outside Roger's office, ready to go to the courthouse to brief the D.A. Grace was dressed in a long blue dress with white blouse and shoes. From her skimpy wardrobe at Lois's residence, Abbie chose a tan business suit and matching pumps. I looked like a country preacher, wearing the wrinkled suit I had worn at Hugh's funeral.

"Betty, please tell the Chief we're here."

"Like some fresh coffee while you wait?" she offered.

"Thanks, Betty," Abbie replied. "We would love it but we must hit the road to the courthouse. We have a ten o'clock appointment with the D.A. Rain check?"

"You got it, even if it never rains again in Comal County."

Gripping a brief case, Chief Rogers burst out of his office with a "Let's go, folks."

"Don't let this guy buffalo you," Rogers cautioned, once we were seated in the SUV. "He growls but doesn't bite. We not only outnumber him, we're going to outfox him as well. Thanks to Ms. Woodley, we have great evidence to present."

"Yesterday I was Grace," she said from the back seat. "Why am I 'Ms. Woodley' today, sir?"

Rogers chuckled. "I apologize! How may I regain your good graces, Grace?" We tittered at his question.

We endured the obligatory wait period once we reached the hallway outside the D.A. office. There were a dozen gilded photos of previous District Attorneys on the wall. Our scheduled time of 10:00 had passed when the outer door opened and we were allowed inside.

The D.A., Winslow Brackett, studied us as we filed into his sanctum.

"Good to see you again, Chief," he bluffed. "Didn't know you were bringing an entourage."

Chief Rogers introduced each of us and we were allowed to sit in a row of chairs beside the D.A.'s big desk.

"Will this take long?" Brackett asked. "I have an important court case at eleven," he said, glancing at his Rolex.

"We are about to present new evidence concerning the recent murder of Mr. Hugh Grimes," Chief Rogers began. "We have not only the sworn testimony of a witness about the murder plan, we brought the witness!"

"She is Ms. Grace Woodley, of Canyon Lake. Her testimony is so concise. I suggest you read her testimony which clearly incrim…"

The D.A. interrupted Rogers. "I'm certain, Chief Rogers, that, I can discern by myself what the testimony reveals.

"Give me a moment to read it."

The D.A. coughed, leaned forward, adjusted his glasses, and read Grace's sworn statement. Not once, but twice.

He studied Grace, alert and facing him, sitting straight in her chair.

"Ms., uh, Woodley, did you freely make this sworn statement without any offer of remuneration?"

"I did, sir,"

He referred to the statement. "Did you clearly hear the man identified in your statement, ask, 'Do you mean, I am free to handle him as I see fit?"

"Yes, I clearly heard him say those words," Grace replied.

"Ms. Woodley, I have the same question for you concerning the woman's reply, 'Do as you please, but I want no fallout on me, the estate or the insurance policies. Understood?"

"That's exactly what she said, sir. I have excellent hearing."

The D.A. sat back in his chair and stared at the ceiling "In your opinion, Ms. Woodley, what did the woman mean by that?"

"I think it clear, sir, that she instructed the man to handle her husband as he saw fit, to include killing him, providing his death did not involve the woman, the estate or insurance policies."

The D.A. turned to the second page of the statement. "What do you think was the man's purpose in insisting the woman repeat that she did not know the location of her husband's favorite fishing spot?"

Grace cleared her throat "The man--let's say his name, Don Drake--did not want the woman--Mrs. Grimes--suspected of her husband's murder since she didn't even know about the place where the murder was committed."

"And why the man's insistence that the woman keep as a permanent record' that cancelled check?"

Grace cleared her throat again. I handed her a glass of water which she sipped before answering.

"They wanted to make it appear that Don Drake had completed the security job he was hired to perform by Mrs. Grimes. She had paid the bill, concluding his services."

The D.A. wiped his forehead with a sleeve.

"And what about the man's insistence that he and the woman have absolutely no contact for six months?"

"To make it appear that their relationship was strictly professional and had ended."

Grace paused. "In actuality, this man and woman planned to go on a vacation cruise together after the six months no-contact period. By then, the public's memory of the husband's murder would be muddled if not forgotten. By then, she also could redeem the value of her dead husband's life insurance policy, if she chose."

The D.A. pressed his hands to his forehead. "Your testimony, Ms. Woodley, is convincing to me, hopefully to a judge and jury as well, once we're in court.

"I think we can convince the judge to sign arrest warrants, citing conspiracy to commit murder, naming both Mrs. Grimes and Mr. Drake.

The D.A. wiped his brow again. "Chief, will you provide me with their full names and addresses for the warrants? If all goes well, the warrants could be issued by tomorrow noon, served early tomorrow afternoon and the pre-trial session scheduled for early next week.

"I think it most advisable, Chief Rogers, that you institute an immediate witness protection, program. Ms. Woodley could be in grave danger from reprisals. These people are apparently quite dangerous."

"Yes, sir. I'll take care of that." Rogers looked at Grace. "I'll protect her myself if necessary."

"You mean, if I asked," she quipped.

THIRTY SIX

CANYON LAKE

SATURDAY

"What about us? Abbie rotated in the D.A. visitor chair until she looked me in the eye. "What do we do now?"

"Cut and run." I replied. I hadn't thought of a better answer yet.

"I can't believe you said that!" Abbie's eyes blazed at me for an instant, making me pause.

"Let's get out of here and go someplace for coffee and serious talk," I suggested.

"Okay" she replied as we left the D.A. office and retrieved the SUV downstairs.

"What about Grace?" she asked.

"If you didn't notice, our police chief has taken a shine to Grace. They'll be alright."

Those big blue eyes blinked at me. "Are you sure?"

"Trust me. She's in very good hands and seems happy to be there."

We ended up at the Country Kitchen again, staring at each other, stirring coffee and ordering fish tacos and hot sauce.

Abbie held up a finger. "Here's what I'm thinking. One. We return to her place and tell Lois she's about to be arrested and help her get away, fast."

I also held up a finger. "Two, we'd be guilty of a crime if we did that. Maybe you're that anxious to again be cellmates with Lois, like in college?"

"Think harder," she punched me. "Lois is my friend and we need to assist her."

"Okay, let's hand her a ticket to Dallas and help her on the bus."

"Quit that!" she snapped "We've got to do something!"

Our 'something' turned out to be returning to Lois' mansion and lie. We told her we were going home to catch up with our businesses. What we actually did, was retrieve a few essentials from upstairs and find a local motel where we would brain-storm a better solution for Lois.

Once at her residence, we found Eloise and Lois happily sitting on the terrace having tea. Lois waved us over. "Come sit down."

We attempted happy faces and joined them on big, padded chairs. Eloise left for more cups while Abbie and I studied a suddenly changed, much happier Lois. She wore a revealing wraparound topped by a silk shirt, all in her now-favorite shade of hot red.

She fluffed her hair, also bright red, and winked at me. "Ask me, Bruno! Come on, ask me! You're dying to know, aren't you? Confess!"

Lois laughed at my blank look.

"The red bra and panties! I can hear your brain tumblers clicking away.

"Yes, yes, I'm wearing them right now!" She answered herself.

"No more drab little Lois. I'm a new WOMAN!"

THIRTY SEVEN

SAN ANTONIO

SATURDAY

No one ever burst into Mr. Drake's private office but Clive, his assistant did, that afternoon. "Mr. Drake, please come with me now! We must leave for the airport immediately! I've booked you a flight to Mexico City!"

Drake studied his usually quiet, no-nonsense assistant.

"Why am I going to Mexico, Clive?"

"Sir, something terrible happened at the county courthouse this morning! You've got to leave immediately before you are arrested!"

The last word caught Drake's attention. He sat straight in his chair. Never had he faced arrest during his long, not entirely legal, career. Arrest would blight his proud reputation as well as damage his income.

"Sit down, Clive, take a breather and tell me what calamity happened at the courthouse."

Clive remained standing to emphasize the immediacy of the situation.

"Sir, do you remember we formerly employed a night watchman named Amos? Amos left us after several years for a job as a county constable, serving warrants all over town.

"Luckily, we maintained a close relationship with Amos, despite his official, new duties. Amos just called to tell me that he and a Deputy have been ordered to serve an arrest warrant on you today, in a matter of hours!"

"That's absurd!" Drake laughed. "What are the charges against me?"

"Amos read me the warrant, sir. You are charged with conspiring to commit the murder of Hugh Grimes!

"Here is your first-class ticket to Mexico City. The flight leaves at 12:45, just two hours from now." Clive wiped his forehead with a damp sleeve.

Drake jumped to his feet, cursing. "That damned Grimes woman must have admitted to the D.A. we planned her husband's death!

"Damn her! She couldn't keep her big, red-painted mouth closed, could she?"

Drake sat down. "Clive, bring me a double Scotch on the rocks, please. I'm not going anywhere until payoff with that bitch is complete.

"Also, alert my driver. We're going to Canyon Lake in a few minutes to settle my score with Mrs. Lois Grimes, then to the airport.

"Clive, give Amos $1,000 for his information about the warrant. We want to keep him on tap as our secret informer.

"Get me arrested, will she?"

By 11.30 that morning, Drake sat in the back seat of his Mercedes. With binoculars he studied the front door of the Grimes residence, some 100 yards away. Beside him on the back seat, he checked a loaded deer rifle and scope.

The front door of the residence remained closed.

Drake glanced at his Rolex. Each second seemed like a minute. His impatience grew as the estimated time for his get-away to the airport, thence Mexico City, approached.

With a curse, he got out of the car and asked the driver for his pistol.

Pistol in hand, Drake hurried to the front door and knocked loudly.

In several minutes, the door opened and Lois stood there in her new red outfit, blinking in the strong sunlight.

"Why, Don…What are…"

He glared at her, raising the pistol. "You told the D.A., didn't you, and tried to get me arrested!

"You and your big plans! Well, here's your payoff, Lois!"

The shot echoed throughout the residence. She fell, shot in the open mouth, red lips permanently parted.

Drake raced back to the Mercedes. He growled at the driver. "Let's see if you can get me to the airport and on my flight in less than an hour! There's a bonus if you do it!"

THIRTY EIGHT

CANYON LAKE

SATURDAY

Abbie and I sat at our favorite table in the Cheese Barrel restaurant down town. We had just ordered and were sipping our first coffee. It was much better than the coffee served at the motel where we spent Saturday night together.

No, not exactly together. I was relegated to the couch beside the TV. She claimed the bedroom. Of course, I complied. She's still the boss.

We were enjoying our first coffee of the day when interrupted by loud voices at the next table.

"Did you hear about the murder last night?

"Where? Chicago, again?"

"No. Right here in Canyon Lake. I heard it on the police scanner all night long. Someone shot a lady at the front door of her home. Sounds like Chicago or Dallas, right?"

"Did they identify the lady?"

"Sure they did. Her name's Granns, or something like that."

At this, Abbie upset her coffee.

The first voice asked, "Do you mean Grimes?" That's the name of the missing man who burned up in a shack at the lake."

"Okay, Grimes. She must have been his wife."

Abbie jumped up, spilling more coffee on her new sun dress.

"God, Bruno! Did you hear that? Lois was killed! We've get to get out there right away to help poor Eloise. She's there by herself in that big mansion, probably scared and frantic."

We broke speed limits in the SUV all the way to 101 Lake View Drive. Pulling up in the parking lot, we stared at the yellow crime scene tapes festooning the front door. A policeman stood guard there.

"You can't come in here!" the policeman insisted, holding up a hand. "This is a crime scene."

"But we live here."

"You live here?"

"Yes, we do."

He offered a clip board and pen.

"You both must sign this log, listing full names, addresses and telephone numbers. Otherwise, no entry."

Dutifully, we complied, writing our names and addresses on the log.

"Then go in through the terrace, if the maid will admit you."

Abbie turned to the policeman. "How's Eloise doing? Is she okay after the terrible murder of Mrs. Grimes at this front door?"

The policeman shrugged. "You'll have to ask her."

Unable to hold my question any longer, I blurted, "Who killed her?"

The policeman looked at me suspiciously, after reading my name on the log. "Chief Rogers wants you to call him. He's been looking for you for hours."

Inside the residence, Eloise and Abbie hugged each other fiercely.

"Are you alright? I was afraid you'd run away after Lois' was…you know."

Eloise wiped away tears. "She was a wonderful lady. We had the longest talk yesterday morning about my future. Can you imagine?

More tears flowed. "She was concerned about me!"

“I know,” Abbie hugged her again. “We were roommates at college for four years. She was always a very thoughtful person.”

“And generous!” Despite the tears, Eloise held out a document.

“What’s this?”

“She decided to make me the beneficiary of her estate, if anything happened to her. Can you believe it? What a wonderful lady!”

Abbie paused, to open a billfold and hand Eloise a business card. “If you’re ever interested in hearing my plan to refurbish this residence, let me know.”

Eloise grabbed Abbie’s hand. “More immediately, I need assistance in planning a memorial service for Lois. Would you and your assistant help me?”

“I’ll ask him, but I’m sure our answer is yes.”

Meanwhile, Chief Rogers was giving me an earful about Lois’ murder.

“Someone…was it you?” he asked. “Someone warned Drake that an arrest warrant was about to be served on him.”

Shocked, I took a big breath. “Chester, you can’t be serious! Abbie and I were here to help Lois any way we could. How did Drake find out he was going to be served? I don’t know how he did it. It wasn’t Abbie or me!

"Where is he now?" I asked. "Did he get away before the warrant was served?"

Chester conceded. "He did."

"Is Drake the only suspect of Lois' murder?"

"Bingo, Bruno!"

I relaxed slightly from his interrogation, part friendly, part inquisitive.

"Chester, have you already initiated a national manhunt for him, to return him to face a murder charge?"

"Of course, Bruno. But the manhunt is international, not just here. We think he hopped a flight to Mexico as soon as he shot Lois. His office in San Antonio is silent about his whereabouts."

Abbie and I checked out of our motel and back into Lois'--now Eloise's--residence. I took both ladies to a leisurely dinner in San Marcos. The three of us wanted to get away, even for a few hours, from 101 Lake View Drive.

On return, Eloise excused herself, claiming fatigue, leaving Abbie and I on the big terrace. The evening was warm and starry-bright.

"I propose we talk abut us, Abbie," I said.

She grabbed me by the collar and kissed me hard. "About time, cowboy! About time!"

Printed in the United States
by Baker & Taylor Publisher Services